SHAFFER
Shaffer, Andrew,
Hope rides again /

HOPE RIDES AGAIN

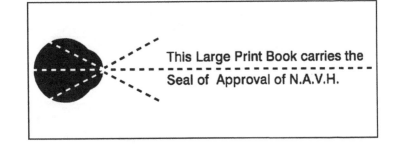

This Large Print Book carries the
Seal of Approval of N.A.V.H.

AN OBAMA BIDEN MYSTERY

HOPE RIDES AGAIN

ANDREW SHAFFER

THORNDIKE PRESS
A part of Gale, a Cengage Company

Farmington Hills, Mich • San Francisco • New York • Waterville, Maine
Meriden, Conn • Mason, Ohio • Chicago

**LIBRARY OF CONGRESS CIP DATA ON FILE.
CATALOGUING IN PUBLICATION FOR THIS BOOK
IS AVAILABLE FROM THE LIBRARY OF CONGRESS**

ISBN-13: 978-1-4328-6657-0 (hardcover alk. paper)

Published in 2019 by arrangement with Quirk Productions, Inc.

Printed in Mexico
1 2 3 4 5 6 7 23 22 21 20 19

To the Windy City,
with love

"MAY THE HINGES OF YOUR FRIENDSHIP
NEVER GO RUSTY."

— Irish proverb

1

What a bunch of malarkey.

That had been my response when I'd seen *Murder on the Amtrak Express* on the paperback rack at the airport. Some two-bit hack had written a potboiler starring yours truly, Joe Biden. Not only that, but the money-grubbing publisher had the gall to slap my mug on the cover. There I was, grimacing behind the wheel of a silver Pontiac Firebird Trans Am — a car I'd never driven in my life. Now, six chapters in, my initial assessment of its literary merit was unchanged. Sometimes you *can* judge a book by its cover.

I might as well have flushed my fifteen bucks down the crapper.

My cab screeched to a halt, sending the book tumbling from my hands. The cabbie — a dead ringer for Bears legend Mike Ditka — laid on the horn. A half dozen pedestrians dashed in front of us, tying up four lanes of bumper-to-bumper traffic on Lake Shore Drive.

Traffic had been stop-and-go since Midway. What should have been a twenty-minute drive into Chicago had already taken double that.

"Is there another route?"

Ditka shook his head. "St. Paddy's Day weekend. Holiday's tomorrow, but the parade's today. Your friend Obama picked da wrong morning for his ecumenical forum, if you ask me."

"Economics," I said. "It's a global *economics* forum."

Ditka glared at me in the rearview mirror. I could tell he wanted to say something smart, but he was having a rough time getting the old hamster to spin the wheel. A woman in a tight pair of green hot pants raced to catch up to her friends, feather boa in tow. My driver redirected his attention accordingly.

I should have expected the zaniness. St. Patrick's Day was the second biggest day on the Irish American calendar, right after November twentieth (birthday of the forty-seventh vice president of the United States). Outside of Boston, there wasn't another American city that took more pride in its Irish heritage than Chicago. By noon, the sidewalks would be stained with Guinness.

We started moving again. I groped around under the front seat for the book. My fingers brushed it, but the cab braked hard and it slipped away. Thank God I hadn't eaten anything this morning. If I had, it would have been all over the backseat. There was a reason most cab seats were vinyl.

"Lose something back there?" Ditka asked, craning his head around as we inched forward. The hedgehog on his upper lip was dotted with spittle.

"Nothing important," I said. The book belonged under the seat. I'd read cereal boxes with better character development. In the parlance of Tony the Tiger, the book was not *grrreat.*

Wave after wave of pedestrians were now jaywalking around us, weaving between cars. Horns honked, with little effect. Traffic had come to a complete standstill.

I couldn't see the Tribune Tower, but I knew it was situated along the river. A mile away, give or take a city block. If I were still in office, I could have arranged a helicopter extraction. Good ol' Marine Two would've gotten me there faster than you could say "Scott Pruitt." Those heady days, however, were long gone — and besides, I'd never taken advantage of my position as a public servant like that.

I glanced at my watch. Quarter till nine. The prayer breakfast would be wrapping up shortly. If I hoofed it from here, I still had a chance to catch the keynote address. I might miss Barack's introduction, but I wasn't in town to see him. Not this time.

I cleared my throat. "Just let me out here."

Ditka shrugged. No sweat off his stones. I paid my fare in cash, stepped out onto the curb. A cool breeze rolled off Lake Michigan. All I had to do was head west until I hit the Magnificent Mile, then turn north. In the midst of a city-wide bar crawl.

"Be careful out there," Ditka shouted through the open door. "It's snake weather."

The Mazda in front of him moved forward three inches, causing a line of cars to honk like mad when the cab didn't follow suit. I threw them a gentle wave, which instigated another chorus of honking. Tough crowd.

"Snake weather, huh?" I said, lingering at the open door.

"Supposed to warm up into da fifties today," Ditka said. "First nice weekend of spring is always the most dangerous. The city thaws, the snakes come out. Pickpockets, swindlers. Gangbangers with itchy trigger fingers. Criminals of every stripe."

A solitary green feather floated past my

face. I batted it away. He might have been yanking my chain, but I didn't think so. There was something in the air. The Midwest had been under a blanket of snow and ice since early December. Three-plus long months of tension simmering below the surface, unleashed by Mother Nature.

I snorted. "Don't worry about me," I told him. "This isn't my first rodeo."

It wasn't until I shut the door that I remembered I'd never been to a rodeo.

2

Every city has its own springtime fragrance. Visit Wilmington and you'll wander into a botanical paradise not unlike my wife's shampoo. Washington would forever be associated in my mind with the sweet smell of blossoming magnolias and cherry trees.

As Chicago thawed that March morning, my nostrils were assaulted with a pungent stew of corned beef, cabbage, and horse manure. It was enough to make me nostalgic for the Senate chambers in August in the seventies, when air-conditioning was still considered a luxury. Back before global warming had made it a necessity.

I ducked into a souvenir store for a little St. Paddy's flair to blend in with the downtown crowd. I was already strapped for time, but I would be in real trouble if anyone recognized me. The last thing I needed was to be engulfed by hundreds upon hundreds of well-wishers chanting "Run, Joe, run!"

I modeled a green-and-white striped scarf in a mirror. Behind me, I caught a glimpse of a short, squat fellow with a reddish chinstrap beard. Green jacket: check. Newsboy cap: check. A damn leprechaun. All he was missing was a pot of gold.

"Next."

The clerk was waving me up to the counter. I turned around, scanning the store for the leprechaun, but there were only a couple of young women snapping photos of each other in four-leaf-clover sunglasses. Huh. I handed the clerk a twenty.

"Keep the change," I said. "I don't need a bag."

His hand was still outstretched. "It's $34.99, sir."

"For a scarf?"

"It's a nice scarf." He motioned to a display of garish green socks adorned with shamrocks and mugs of green beer. Two pairs for ten bucks. "If you're looking for something on the cheap side . . ."

I handed him another twenty.

This time I asked for the change.

Nobody gave me so much as a second look over the next eight city blocks. It wasn't because of the scarf. I was just another white-haired Irish American in a city swimming with Celtic cud chewers. I passed no fewer than twenty-three doppelgängers who could have made good money impersonating me at birthday parties and confirmations.

The sidewalk in front of the Tribune Tower was blocked off with sawhorses — not for the parade, but for the protestors. A small crowd of twenty or thirty Occupy activists were milling about, wielding posters attacking the usual suspects.

NO BORDERS, NO BANKS.

STOP CORPORATE GREED.

MR. OBAMA TEAR DOWN THIS WALL (STREET).

Not exactly the homecoming welcoming committee.

Not exactly surprising, either.

A pair of cops on horseback watched the fracas. They paid no attention as I skirted around them. They were only one line of defense, however. A muscled-up heavy in a too-tight suit was blocking the main entrance doors. Had to be private security. I'd never seen a Secret Service agent with the Van Heusen label still stitched onto their sleeve.

A man in an ivory suit and fedora barreled out of one of the revolving doors. He brushed past the security guard, and I stepped to the side to avoid being bowled over. The man met my eyes as he passed. A VIP pass hung on a lanyard around his thick neck. He wore a look of determination — he had somewhere to be. And by the way his eyebrows were angled, he didn't look too happy about it.

I removed my shades and turned to the guard. An Irish and an American flag were flapping above us in the wind.

"This the conference?" I asked.

"Need to see your pass."

"I should be on the list. Biden. Joe Biden."

Without taking his eyes off me, he loosened the walkie-talkie from his belt like he was unholstering a pistol. "If you're not wearing a pass —"

The revolving door behind him spun again. The woman who emerged was wearing a sharp blue top. I noticed she didn't have a conference pass clipped to it. I had half a mind to ask the guard why this woman didn't need a pass, but I already knew the answer: it was Michelle Obama. And Michelle Obama did whatever the heck Michelle Obama wanted.

3

The Tribune Tower lobby was small but elegant, with tall, cavernous ceilings. A video board welcomed us to THE RISING HOPE CENTER'S FIRST ANNUAL GLOBAL ECONOMICS FORUM — SATURDAY, MARCH 16, 2019. First *annual*? Barack always liked to go big or go home.

"Welcome to Chicago," Michelle said, embracing me. "You're looking good, Joe. Have you lost weight?"

"My doctor tracks all that bunk. I've been hitting the hotel StairMasters pretty hard, though. Life on the road."

Michelle marched us around a metal detector. There were suits everywhere. A couple were well dressed enough to be Secret Service. "You sure picked a wild day to visit Chi-Town," she said. "Surprised the police aren't in riot gear."

"The protestors hardly look like they're going to riot. They look more like they need a ham sandwich and a nap."

"The ones with the signs?" She scoffed. "Barack will spend an hour discussing the resource-based economy and collaborative commons with them later. No, I was talking about the shamrock crowd."

"I wouldn't worry. You've got more muscle here than a Gold's Gym," I said. "And I'm not just talking about your arms."

She playfully slapped at me and led me down an escalator.

"Did I miss him?" I asked.

"Barack? He should be in the green room."

"I meant his pal. Caruso."

"Oh, him," she said. "He's still on stage. We'll swing by there and you can peek in."

A week ago, Barack had called me out of the blue to say that Caruso, a rapper turned social-justice activist with strong ties to Chicago's African American community, was delivering the opening keynote at today's event. If I was serious about running for president — and serious about winning — this was somebody I needed to meet. There'd been a lot of talk since 2016 about winning back White America. Here was a chance to hear firsthand about the issues facing Black America. Barack would be in and out of the conference all day, but

Caruso had agreed to sit down with me for a private one-on-one after his speech. I couldn't ride Barack's coattails forever when it came to minority outreach, especially since he wasn't likely to stump for anyone in the Democratic primaries. Not even someone he'd traded friendship bracelets with.

Michelle and I stopped at a pair of double doors where a black teenager was standing, hands clasped in front of him. He was dressed in a crisp white shirt and black slacks, like a Jehovah's Witness. You could see your reflection in his polished shoes.

"You're welcome to catch the rest of the speech from the back of the room," Michelle explained to me. "He's supposed to wrap up" — she looked at her Apple Watch — "in fifteen minutes. You might want to cut out early and head to the green room."

"The green room. That must be for St. Patrick's Day, right?"

"What do you mean?" she asked.

"I meant because it's green and . . . never mind."

"Oh, I get it, Joe. I get it." She turned to the teen by the door. "Can you show Mr. Biden to the green room when he's ready?"

The kid hesitated. "I'm not supposed to leave my post, ma'am."

20

"I'll send another volunteer down to take over as usher. You're almost off anyway, right?"

"Got to get to work at the freight yard by eleven."

"We'll get you there." She turned to me. "Joe, this is Shaun Denton. He's part of our Rising Stars program. The next generation of community leaders, homegrown right here in Chicago. Shaun and the rest of the volunteers here are from Pastor Brown's church." A call came in for her. "If you'll excuse me."

It was just the kid and me. I shook his hand and introduced myself. He looked a little star-struck, believe it or not. I liked him already. "Where your shades at?" he asked.

"My aviators? Let's see . . ." I pretended to pat down my pockets and then, voilà, I whipped them out of my jacket. "Wanna try 'em on?"

He grinned. "Pretty fly," he said, modeling my glasses. "I seen you before. At Grant Park. Eleven years ago."

"Election night. You must have been a baby."

"Ma took me. First black president and all. Said she wouldn't believe it unless she saw it with her own eyes. I'm glad she lived to see it."

When he removed my aviators, his eyes were wet. "I read your book," he said as he folded my sunglasses carefully, something to do so he didn't have to make eye contact. "The whole thing." He sounded a little sheepish about that, but I could only grin like a fool.

"You did?"

"Had to do a report for school. There were all these copies at the Rising Hope Center. Mrs. Obama brought them in for us."

My heart grew a size at that. I made a mental note to buy a couple copies of *Becoming* and leave them in the waiting room at my dentist's.

"Hope you liked it," I said.

He nodded. "The way you took that train home every night, all the way from DC just to be with your kids. That was cool, man. Nobody'd walk two blocks down the sidewalk for me." He laughed like it didn't hurt to say that, but I could see it hurt. Hurt to say. Hurt to hear.

"If you were my son," I said, "I'd take an Amtrak round the world and back for you."

He smiled like he thought I was full of it, but I meant it. I really did. Kid like that, I just wanted to take him home with me to

Jill and the grandkids, let him spend some time with the Bidens, see what a real family was like.

"Here." Shaun tried to hand my aviators back to me. "Thanks."

"Keep 'em," I said with a wink. "I got a spare."

Michelle came back and Shaun returned to his post, aviators on, looking like a junior Secret Service agent. "Wish I could stick around, but I've got to be going," she said. "Brunch with Oprah. I know you're leaving later today, but I'm sure we'll have plenty of time to catch up this summer."

"Or you could skip brunch and hang out now."

She flashed me a look of severe incredulity, a look she'd flashed me hundreds of times over the years.

"Kidding," I said with a grin. Then, more seriously: "Is she here?"

"You don't think all this security is for me and Barack, do you?"

I'd never met Oprah before, so I had no idea what kind of security she rolled with. She'd recently done a couple fundraisers for Democrats. There was chatter she might even make a run for president. If that happened, I was going to be in for a dogfight.

After Michelle was gone, I listened to

Caruso, my back against the wall. His hair was long and braided. He was tall as a cornstalk in August, and spoke with a slow Midwestern drawl that turned his words into poetry.

". . . the gulf between the richest and poorest in this world is greater than it's ever been at any point in the history of recorded humanity. In the United States alone, the average CEO earns 563 times what the average worker earns. Meanwhile, the average worker's spending power has dwindled over the past forty years, causing the American middle class to crater. We're not alone. Around the world, poverty . . ."

I caught myself nodding along with the audience. The kids outside with signs weren't protestors, I realized — they were fans. Not necessarily of President Obama, but definitely of the man onstage. I wanted to hear more of his speech. Unfortunately, I couldn't get Oprah out of my mind. She wasn't listed as a conference speaker. She didn't live in Chicago these days. Was she here to meet with Caruso as well? One thing was certain: Oprah was here for more than two-for-one mimosas.

4

I'd been on the road for the past eighteen months, stumping for Democratic candidates and promoting my book with a series of town-hall-style events. A trial balloon for 2020 that fooled nobody. I'd been back to Delaware for a couple weeks following the midterms, but ever since hitting the road again in January, I'd spent only a handful of nights in my own bed. A quick sojourn with Jill in St. Croix had only reminded me of the distance between us.

If family was a slowly fading memory kept alive by Facebook and Skype, then friends were ghosts of the past. Barack and I still kept in touch, but he knew that I had to keep the pedal to the metal. There wasn't time to hang out like in the old days, when we'd met weekly for lunch. The last time I'd seen him was a ski trip around Christmas. President W. had been in Aspen as well, and even joined us on the slopes for an hour or two before retiring to the club-house with Michelle for hot cocoa with marshmallows.

I hadn't planned on seeing Barack until this summer, when our families would be vacationing together at Rehoboth Beach. I was in Chicago for one day, with no expectations that our schedules would sync up. When Michelle had said there was a chance I could catch him in the green room, how-ever, my heart started racing. He had that effect on me.

He had that effect on everyone.

Unfortunately, when I entered the green room, Barack wasn't there. My first clue should have been the lack of Secret Service agents at the door. Some detective I was. I thanked Shaun and sent him on his way. He had to get to work. Plus, he'd already been introduced to President Obama earlier that morning.

Like most makeshift green rooms, this one was a small conference room dressed up with a portable clothing rack and a few couches. There was also a cloth-covered banquet table with the requisite cheese and fruit spread. No crackers, though. There were never any crackers.

I picked up a copy of the conference schedule. There was a VIP reception that evening in the Crown foyer. Twenty-fifth floor. I hadn't been invited, even though I was the guy who put the "VP" in VIP. Not that it mattered. My plane would be taking off as it started. It was back to Delaware —

A flash of movement underneath the banquet table caught my eye. I spotted the soles of two black shoes poking out from beneath the draped tablecloth. A terrorist planting a bomb?

There was a grunt from under the table. The shoes started backing up. Whoever was under there was coming out. I balled my hands into fists and put my dukes up, ready to rumble.

"Come out slowly, with your hands in the air," I said. "No funny business."

The creeping creeper paused. The shoes were large, the slacks tan and pressed. I caught a glimpse of tall socks, decorated with shamrocks and mugs of green beer.

"I can't back up with my hands in the air." Though muffled, the deep baritone was unmistakable.

I lowered my fists. "Come on out, Mr. President."

Barack Obama stood and brushed off his slacks and matching tan suit jacket. When he'd worn the same ensemble as president, he'd been ridiculed by both the right and the left. It was too casual, too bland. An ophthalmologist wrote an op-ed warning that the suit's pancake-batter coloring "was an affront to the optic nerve" that could "trigger neurogenic inflammation in susceptible individuals." One House member went so far as to say the suit was a national security risk. I'm not kidding, folks. Seeing Barack in the suit again, I was surprised to discover it wasn't as hideous as I'd remembered it.

It was worse.

"Hey, Joe," Barack said, smothering me in a bear hug. I patted him on the back. The bromance was alive and well. "Nice scarf. Where'd you bury the body of the leprechaun you stole it from?"

"Really? You're going to lecture me on my sartorial choices while —"

A huffing, puffing Secret Service agent barreled into the room. Unlike the rest of the agents, this one was a known quantity. Steve. I'm sure he had a last name — he was no Cher — but I'd never known anyone to use it. Last I'd heard, he'd been promoted to the White House's tactical detail. I wasn't surprised to see him back on Obama's detail, though. I'd had a feeling he wasn't going to last long inside the current administration. Nobody does.

"Steve." I started to go in for a hug but decided on a handshake.

He ignored my outstretched hand. "What the hell is going on?" he fumed. "I relieved the agent outside the door, poked my head in, and there was nobody in here. I spent the past five minutes hunting for a missing POTUS, and I get back here and —"

"Slow down, Steve," Barack said. "Nobody's missing. Nobody got hurt."

"There's scuff marks on the knees of your pants, sir," Steve said. "Were you wrestling on the floor?"

"You still on the whole low-carb diet?" I asked Steve.

His expression went from angry and perplexed to just plain angry. "I was never on a low-carb diet. It was a zero-carb diet. It wasn't sustainable. I've gone paleo."

"The caveman diet."

"It's not all raw saber-tooth-tiger steaks and mammoth burgers."

"Got some pterodactyl hot wings, too," I joked.

He stared at me. "Pterosaurs were extinct by the Paleolithic Era."

"So that's a no."

"That's a no," he said. He exited with a slam of the door. When he was gone, I asked Barack what in Samhain he'd been doing on his hands and knees under the catering table.

"I misplaced my BlackBerry."

"Under the table?"

"I don't know where I misplaced it. If I knew, then it wouldn't be misplaced."

"You've got the numbers for every world leader in your phone." I paused. "And Bradley Cooper."

"He changed his number."

"Without telling you?"

He closed his eyes and massaged his temples. "I was supposed to give up my phone for Lent. I was good for a couple of weeks, but then I started sneaking it out to check basketball scores. And then read the paper. And pretty soon I'd fallen off the wagon completely." He looked over at me. "Maybe this is God's way of helping me get back on the wagon."

"Lent? Trying to reconnect with your Irish ancestors?"

"More like trying to reconnect with my family. Michelle wanted me to try going a month without it. Said she 'wanted her husband back.' "

Not only had I not realized it was St. Paddy's this Sunday until the cabbie mentioned it, but I hadn't given anything up for Lent this year. When you don't drink or smoke, you don't have much to give up. I couldn't even give up coffee because the last time I'd partaken of the roasted bean was in college. I could give up ice cream, though I'd rather give up breathing. Still, I had to marvel at Barack: he was a better Irish Catholic than Joe Biden.

A vibrating phone broke the silence, startling me half out of my penny loafers. I patted my pocket. The buzz wasn't coming from my phone. It was coming from a checkered suit jacket on the clothes rack.

"It's someone else's phone," Barack said. "I already checked."

"Have you checked your own pockets?"

Barack cocked his head.

"One time I thought I lost my wallet," I said. "Looked all over the damned Eisenhower for it. You know where it was?"

"Where was it, Joe?"

"In my front pocket!" I said with a laugh. "See, I usually put it in my back pocket. I'd had it the whole time, but in the wrong pocket. I have no idea how it got there, either."

"Maybe you put it there."

He might have been right.

He usually was.

Barack explained that the last time he'd seen his phone was that morning, when he'd set it down in the green room next to the fruit and cheese tray. Michelle had come in, and he'd stuffed it under a plate. Then he'd gone to the prayer breakfast. He hadn't remembered the phone until later. By that time, any number of people could have come and gone from the room.

"Let me see your phone, Joe," he said. "If I can log onto the BlackBerry website, I can pinpoint the phone's location and . . ."

His voice faded as I showed him my phone.

"A flip phone? Every time I see you, Joe, you look the same, but your phone gets older and older."

"It's got a couple of apps. An Internet browser from the last century. The whole thing's harder to work than a damn VCR, if you ask me. That's how I like it, though."

He poked his head outside and asked Steve to find him a laptop.

"There's a whole platter of cheese here," Barack said, returning. "Have at it."

"They expect you to eat all that? With no crackers?"

"Oh, Lord, no. Oprah was in here earlier, but she didn't touch a thing. Pastor Brown, now there's an eater. He can eat even you under the table — except he didn't eat much at breakfast either, come to think of it. Too bad. They had these bagels, the hard kind that you can only find at New York delis. The kind you like."

It was for the best that I hadn't crashed the breakfast. I wouldn't have been able to work up much of an appetite around Barack's tan suit. It was too close in color to baby spit-up.

"Oprah was in here," I said absently.

"That's right. Everything OK, Joe? You seem distracted."

"Was she in here before or after your phone went missing?"

"You think Oprah stole my phone," he said. "Oprah."

Barack didn't appreciate my obvious joke. Besides, even if we discovered the smoking gun in Oprah's handbag, no jury would ever convict her. Privately, I wondered if she was as big a saint as everybody believed she was. Heck, plenty of people thought I was some sort of boy scout, when in reality my farts stunk like everyone else's. Sometimes worse than everyone else's. I should have never had that battered onion plate last night.

Steve knocked on the door. He'd found us a desktop computer upstairs.

Barack glanced at his watch. "It took you twenty minutes. In the Tribune Tower. Isn't there, like, an entire floor filled with newspaper reporters with computers?"

"There is," Steve said, "but if I marched you into the newsroom, it would take the rest of the afternoon to muscle you out of there. You know how the media loves you, sir."

I nodded. "They sure do."

Barack frowned at me.

"Don't pretend to be mad," I said.

Barack sighed. "Caruso told me he'd stop in here after his presentation. Probably got held up signing autographs. In the meantime, you want to tag along with me, Joe? Shouldn't take too long. I know you're something of a detective these days."

He was ribbing me about *Murder on the Amtrak Express,* which I would never admit to him to having picked up. He didn't understand the appeal of pulp fiction. "Low-brow," he called it. He was fond of saying he had a big brain and needed to feed it big food. We both knew that if I'd been a real detective, I wouldn't have gotten us both almost killed two summers ago. If I'd been a real detective, I would have solved the mystery of my friend Finn Donnelly's death before more bodies piled up around Wilmington. I was no flatfoot; I was a politician.

That didn't mean I wasn't game for some Hardy Boys hijinks.

5

The president's BlackBerry is missing.

If this were a potboiler-of-the-week starring Charles Bronson, those five words would have kicked off a city-wide manhunt for the culprit. But this was real life. This was No Drama Obama. His phone might have been missing, but he was as cool, calm, and collected as ever. Over the years I'd seen his thick veneer crack only a handful of times, when there was much more on the line than a missing phone.

"Can you think of any enemies, anyone who would want to steal your phone?" I asked in the elevator.

Barack twisted his mouth to the side. "Come to think of it, I *was* wondering what Sean Hannity was doing here."

"Forget I said anything."

He laughed. "You're getting worked up over nothing, Joe. I bet Michelle swiped it, to teach me a lesson. I'll log onto the website, track it, and I bet you eighty-three dollars that it's around the corner where she's having brunch."

"Eighty-three dollars?"

The elevator stopped on the first floor.

"That's how much I have in my wallet," Barack said.

Steve led us to the lobby. He was a few paces ahead.

"Feels good to get the ol' gang back together," I said. "You, me, well, we're more like a two-man gang, aren't we?"

"Unless you count Steve," Barack said.

"Sure," I mumbled.

"He's the lead agent on my detail now," Barack said. I didn't like being babysat at my age, but the Secret Service was nice to have around sometimes. Like when you needed to make change for a twenty.

We arrived at a small room off to the side of the lobby. One of two desks was occupied by a middle-aged woman with curly hair and dark roots. She looked up from her screen and then returned her gaze to whatever she was working on. Then she did a double-take.

Barack smiled. Between his clenched teeth, he hissed at Steve, "The building's leasing office?"

"You wanted a computer."

The woman — fully flushed now — was staring at the president, mouth agape. A sparrow could've flown right into that maw, laid a couple of eggs, and flown out again without her noticing.

"Checking the basketball scores," Barack said breezily as he sat down across from her. Steve gave her the stink eye and she left in a hurry. He pressed a finger to his earpiece and then turned to us. "That was the front desk. *Nada.* They'll call if someone turns it in."

"Did you tell them whose it was?" Barack asked. "We don't want to turn this into a scene."

"I told them it was Joe's," he said, winking at me.

"Ha-ha," I said. Barack smirked, but we both knew my days of being a national punchline were long past. I hadn't made a public gaffe in at least a week.

I took the seat at the woman's desk and jiggled the mouse. The screensaver went away. "Think I can check my email from here? It's not my WhiteHouse.gov account," I said, then added under my breath, "I don't have access to that anymore."

"These are public computers," Barack said. "You don't know who has been using them. There are probably just as many viruses on the keyboards as there are in the operating system —"

"I'm in," I said as my Yahoo inbox popped up.

I scrolled through the messages — the spam, the scams, and, I guess, a few emails worth reading. Nothing from Jill or the kids. A pleading message from my spokesman, telling me he couldn't hold off the press much longer regarding my 2020 plans. It was time to fish or cut bait.

"That can't be right," Barack said. His brow was furrowed.

I craned my neck to peek at his computer. A red dot pulsated on East Sixty-third Street. A large area labeled NORFOLK SOUTHERN RAILROAD YARD covered the lower half of the map. A freight yard. One of dozens in Chicago. And yet it set off a silent alarm in the back of my mind.

"It says here it's on the South Side," he explained.

"Could it be Michelle?"

"Chez Quis is a few blocks from here, not in Englewood." He clicked the mouse a few times. "There. I've wiped it remotely. Whoever took it has got themselves a very expensive paperweight. Now we can head back downstairs —"

"That's it?"

39

"That's it." Barack stood. "Easy-peasy, Joe."

Easy-peasy? First he stole my Lent; now he was stealing my lines. If my privacy had been violated like his was, I would have been hoppin' mad. We had different philosophies. Different temperaments. Sometimes, I couldn't believe we'd ever become friends at all.

"But — but your phone," I stammered. "Don't you think —"

"I'll get a replacement. It's useless now. If they try to sell it, who would ever believe that it was the president's BlackBerry?"

We left for the elevators. The silent alarm that had been ringing in the back of my mind wouldn't stop, and it had nothing to do with the eighty-three-dollar bet Barack had lost to me (of which I would never see a red cent). I had a good idea who the thief was. Barack was seemingly ready to forget the whole episode, but that was only because he didn't know what I knew.

"I need to get going," I told him. "I remembered I have a thing."

He raised his eyebrows. "What about Caruso? That was kind of why I asked you to town. You'll like him. He's got some great ideas."

"Another time, I'm afraid. My flight leaves

at nine, but I always like to get to the airport early. You never know what those security lines are going to be like."

"You have PreCheck."

I shook my head. "A hundred bucks for five years? I'll stand in the cattle call line with everyone else, thank you very much."

"Still, getting to the airport" — and here he checked his watch — "almost eleven hours early seems excessive."

"I'm putting myself on standby. If I can surprise Jill by getting home early, hey, that's better than a souvenir."

"I'd still buy her a souvenir."

He gave me another bear hug. I still wasn't used to this new, emotional Barack Obama. Ever since I'd leaped in front of a bullet meant for him during our little adventure in 2017, he was the first one to initiate hugs between us.

"See you at the beach this summer?" he said.

"Sounds like a plan, Stan."

What Barack didn't know was that I really did have a plan, and it had nothing to do with stuffing our faces with saltwater taffy on the boardwalk. I was no detective, but you didn't need to be a detective to do detective work. I once replaced the flange inside the toilet in our guest bathroom. That didn't make me a plumber, but I did it. By God, I did it.

To do detective work, all you needed was a clue. Not only did I have that, I also had a suspect: Shaun Denton. And to think I'd trusted him.

6

When I boarded the L, there were only a handful of other passengers. The doors closed and the train rattled and hissed. The bucket seats weren't padded like on Amtrak. Without judgment, I noted that several of my fellow travelers had brought their own padding. The Bidens were not blessed with such ample backsides, however. I settled in for a bumpy ride.

I was headed for the South Side. I anticipated the elevated train would get me there faster than trying to cut back through the parade traffic. Any other time, I wouldn't have gone after the phone — Barack could buy an entire Verizon store's worth of phones if he wanted to. What bugged me was that Shaun had said he was headed to work at a freight yard. Not necessarily the one where Barack's phone had been pinpointed, but it was just too much of a coincidence. A half hour after Shaun leaves for work and the phone just magically appears at a freight yard? There'd been a warning on the computer as Barack wiped the BlackBerry, advising him to contact local law enforcement to track down the device if he suspected it was stolen. "Don't try to retrieve your device on your own," the site warned.

The last thing I wanted was for the police to get involved.

It didn't take a genius-level intellect like Barack Obama's to connect the dots. Shaun seemed like a good kid. He was one of the Obamas' "Rising Stars." If he was indeed the thief, I wanted to give him a chance to do the right thing. Maybe Shaun was pulling my old leg when he said he wished he'd had a dad like me, maybe he wasn't. But if he'd been my son, this is what I'd do — I'd find him and talk some sense into him before he got himself into real trouble.

Slowly, the skyscrapers gave way to single-story brick homes. We stopped every half mile or so to pick up a new crew of working-class Joes and Suzies. I was getting a look at the real Chicago. Most were dressed in service-industry uniforms: checkered chef's pants, polo shirts embroidered with names of fast-food establishments. Comfortable shoes.

Nobody was wearing green except for the baristas.

I debarked at the Sixty-third Street station. My phone's map told me the main entrance to the freight yard was one block south, five blocks east. So this was the South Side. A dangerous area, if you went by the headlines.

I drew in a deep breath and started walking.

I could already feel blisters forming on the bottoms of my feet. That's what you get for tramping around town in dress shoes. If there'd been a CVS along my route, I would have stopped in and picked up some Dr. Scholl's inserts. However, there were only empty lots overtaken by grass on one side of the street, the fenced-in shipping yard on the other. From the elevated station, I'd seen an emerald-green Whole Foods sign a few blocks to the west, looking mighty out of place. Wasn't that the grocer they called "Whole Paycheck"? No way was I buying some organic shoe inserts for double the price. I'd rather walk over broken glass.

And I *was* walking over broken glass. Every five or ten footsteps, something crunched underfoot. A busted bottle. A smashed car window. A picture frame of a happy family with the husband's face cut out. Bad breakup. Maybe Oprah could help.

After a couple of blocks with the sidewalk to myself, I heard the tight patter of footsteps gaining on me. I hugged the concrete wall as I passed under a railroad viaduct, giving whoever was behind me room to pass. When I emerged on the other side, I threw a glance over my shoulder. Nobody there.

Paranoia? Or something else? Had Barack sent the Secret Service to follow me? Perhaps, once upon a time, I'd have worried about that. But Barack and I didn't keep stuff from each other anymore. It was an unspoken agreement, one that I was breaking right now. I'd tell him about Shaun. Eventually. When the time was right.

A cop car with its lights and sirens blaring rounded the corner of a side street, skidding along the road and nearly careening into a crosswalk light. In the distance, another siren whined — this one longer, deeper — and another cop buzzed past.

There was nothing around here to speak of but the yards. We were all on our way to the same place.

Up ahead, trouble was brewing: three police cruisers were blocking the entrance to the freight yard. A fire truck was parked at an angle across one side of the street.

A crowd of gawkers had gathered on the sidewalk. All African American. Meanwhile, I was white as a gravestone in the moonlight. With the scarf, I probably looked to them like I'd just come from a rugby match. At a pub.

Had Barack or the Secret Service tipped off the police about the location of the stolen phone? It seemed unlikely because, in practical terms, Barack was right: it was a paperweight now that it had been wiped and locked. Barack didn't want any publicity, understandably. His mind was on the forum. I seemed to be the only one even mildly worked up about the theft, and that was only because I had a suspect in mind.

On the other hand, I knew that it was too much to believe the police presence here was unrelated to my current quest. They didn't send out this many first responders for some kid who'd imbibed too much green beer and face-planted into the grass.

I shoved my scarf into an overstuffed trash can and entered the huddle.

7

The police officer standing guard at the entrance had a frown on her face too well-worn to be anything but permanent. There weren't any sawhorses or crime scene tape restricting the area, however, so I slipped through the crowd.

She looked me up and down as I approached her. "You a Fed?"

"What makes you say that?" I asked, my voice full of more gravel than a rock pit.

"You all dress the same. Except you . . . you look familiar."

"Some people say I look like Cary Grant."

The officer — Rudin, according to the name patch sewn onto her shirt — looked at me sideways. She turned on her radio. "I got a Mr. Cary Grant out here. Should I send him in?" While she was waiting for a response, she whispered to me, "Which agency?"

"Well —"

Her radio squawked back. It was undecipherable to me, but Rudin seemed to understand whoever was on the other end.

"What'd they say?" I asked.

"They told me they don't care if you're the president of the United States, you're not contaminating their crime scene."

"What if I was the vice president?"

"Not even if you were Cary Grant. You can read all about what happened here in the paper tomorrow. Or maybe not. This is gonna be one of those days. They might simply tally the number of shootings and leave it at that."

"There was a shooting here."

The officer narrowed her eyes. Perhaps she'd realized she'd said too much, or finally recognized that I was putting her on. The look on her face said she was about to toss me like a can of corn.

Right inside the gates, an ambulance was parked with its back doors open. Two EMTs were wheeling a gurney across the pavement from between two shipping containers. The victim's face was partially obscured by an oxygen mask. He had dark skin and black slacks. He was shirtless, but if I had to guess, he'd been wearing a starched white shirt. I had a feeling in my stomach like I'd swallowed a dumbbell.

49

Rudin traced my eyes to the gurney. "Shot twice in the gut. Clean shots, though. He's lucky."

"Think you'll catch who did it?" I said, assuming they hadn't already.

It was a good assumption.

"We've got some shoe prints, which we'll match to the perp when we catch him. You can always pray for video, but there aren't a lot of CCTV cameras around here — the yard's too massive to surveil every inch. A hundred and sixty acres. Something goes missing, insurance deals with it. It is what it is. If we're really, really lucky, we can lift the shooter's fingerprints off the bullet casings, but how often do you get lucky in this business?"

"Not often enough," I said, taking a wild guess. "Any witnesses?"

She gave me a knowing look. "Nobody wants to insert themselves into the middle of a potential gang war, which is what most of these cases shake out to be. That's a one-way ticket to Slab City."

The victim had just arrived at work, she explained. No coworkers saw anything. Unless there was a major break in the case, it didn't sound like there was any hope. The department had their hands full this weekend. Bad things happen, she said.

My nausea returned in a sudden rush — not because of her jaded attitude, but because I had to know. I had to know if it was Shaun.

"Say," Rudin said, adjusting her cap, "which agency did you say you were with?"

"I didn't," I said, breaking through the invisible perimeter. I went straight for the gurney, which the EMTs were loading into the ambulance. I didn't need to pull the oxygen mask from his face to know it was Shaun. It was his shoes — his polished shoes that gave him away.

"Shaun," I said, not that he could hear me.

I didn't care if he'd stolen Barack's BlackBerry or every one of Tom Brady's six Super Bowl rings — the kid didn't deserve this. Nobody did.

"We need some room here," said one of the medics, a young woman with tattooed forearms.

I stepped out of the way. "Hey, you didn't find a BlackBerry on him, did you?"

"Check with your friends," she said, jerking her thumb toward a trio of uniformed cops surrounding the crime scene a couple of car lengths away. The shipping containers on either side of them were decorated with eagles carrying American flags. The cement

51

at the cops' feet was black with dried blood.

The other medic was fiddling with a lever on the gurney. I was in their way, but they were used to guys like me getting in their way. I could tell they were tired of it. Tired of guys like me, tired of treating gunshot victims. Tired of the whole damn thing.

"Found an iPhone," the male medic said without looking up at me.

"That's it?"

His partner hopped into the back of the ambulance with Shaun. I couldn't remember who the patron saint of shooting victims was, so I sent up a prayer to all the saints. Maybe one of them would get the message.

The medic slammed the door shut. "That's all he had in his pockets, besides his wallet. An iPhone."

"Somebody shot him but didn't take his wallet or his phone. What happened to no honor among thieves?"

The medic fired up a cigarette. "Wasn't a robbery. They fired six shots, from far enough away that they missed most of 'em. Somebody wanted him dead." He paused. "You aren't from Chicago."

"Wilmington."

"People don't get shot in Wilmington?"

"They do," I admitted. "All the time."

"Same shit, different zip code. Am I right?"

He climbed into the cab of the ambulance, cigarette dangling from his lips. The ambulance pulled out, siren blaring like an air raid horn. It barely registered over the other sounds of the freight yard: the train whistles, the constant squealing of brakes like nails on a chalkboard. The shooting hadn't slowed down the shipping business at all.

My eyes wandered and found a pair of mirrored shades on the ground, the frames split in half, the plastic lenses crushed to bits by one of the ambulance's tires. I crouched down. Without even reading the Ray-Ban logo on the frames, I knew they were mine. Or they had been mine. Interesting detail about the phone and wallet not being stolen. If the shooter never got close enough to empty Shaun's pockets, then where was the BlackBerry? It had been nearby, around the time of the shooting. That much I could piece together. If Shaun hadn't had it on him, however, that meant that somebody else had swiped the phone from the green room . . . and there was only one "somebody else" in the picture at the moment: the shooter. What sort of mess had I stepped into the middle of?

"Long way from Delaware, Joe."

My body went rigid. Without turning to see who'd crept up on me, I said, "Hello, Rahm."

8

Before I'd even shaken newly elected Illinois Senator Barack Obama's hand, I'd known what he was all about. He was from Chicago, where Democrats had built one of the most corrupt political machines in the country. There's an old joke that goes something like, "Uncle Frank was a conservative until the day he died in Chicago. Since then, he's voted Democrat."

Ipso fatso, Barack was dirtier than the Delaware River.

I couldn't have been more wrong.

Unfortunately, I wasn't so sure about his friends. Rahm Emanuel — a firecracker with the mouth of a sailor — was the cleanest of the bunch, if that tells you anything. To say that we rubbed each other the wrong way would be a gross understatement. We got along like two sticks being used to start a campfire.

"Take us around the block," Rahm told

his driver. "The long way."

Rahm was riding up front with his SUV limo driver. I was sitting in back beside a thick slice of roast beef named Benny Polaski, who'd worked muscle for Barack in 2008. Polaski was a common surname in Chicago, a city with the largest Polish community in the States. At one point, the Irish and Polish hadn't been too friendly. After an influx of African Americans during the Great Migration, suddenly the differences between the Irish and Polish minorities seemed, well, minor.

After a few blocks riding in awkward silence, Rahm finally spoke. "You're going to miss the parade, Joe. It starts in less than an hour."

"Never been much of a parade guy. I like the ones where they throw candy, but I'm too old to fight for it with the kids these days."

"If I'd known you were in town, I could have gotten you a good spot. Cleared all the kiddies out. All the candy you could pick up." He sighed. "I'm supposed to be on the first float, you know. Being the mayor and all."

"Something else come up?"

Rahm glared at me in the rearview. "I got a text from the chief of police saying Joe

Biden was snooping around a crime scene. Joe Biden! On the South Side, for Chrissakes. As if I don't have enough to worry about this weekend as it is." He shook his head. "Listen, you and I have never been friends, but we don't have to be enemies."

He was right. We were never friends. "President Obama invited me to his little economic pow-wow," I said. "I was there this morning. A tad dry. Thought I'd kill a few hours before leaving town by riding the L. I didn't expect to stumble into a crime scene."

"I wouldn't expect you to, either," Rahm said. "Did you read that book? *Murder on the Amtrak Express?*"

"I've been busy."

"It's not bad. Better than that Clinton and Patterson train wreck, if you'll forgive the pun." He paused. "If that crack gets back to Bill, you're toast."

"My lips are sealed."

Rahm chuckled. "I hope you'll forgive me for kidnapping you, by the way."

"Is that what this is?"

Rahm twisted in his seat to look at me. "Does President Obama know you decided to tour one of our economically diverse, industrial-opportunity corridors?"

I shook my head. Polaski unwrapped a

Werther's Original. For himself; he wasn't sharing.

Rahm lowered his voice: "I know what you're doing down here."

"You do?"

"Uh-huh," he said. He turned back around and looked at me in the rearview, wearing a smarmy grin. That was sort of his default expression.

I'd never been a good liar, but now I was going to have to pull a rabbit the size of the Easter Bunny out of my rear. A painful metaphor that made me shift uncomfortably.

He laughed. "I'm kidding you, man." He spread an arm, gesturing out the passenger window to the Norfolk Southern yards. "This is where the magic happens."

"The magic?"

"Chicago is the country's number-one hub for rail traffic. Always has been, always will be. Thirteen hundred trains a day. If you're into trains, like I am — and I know you are, Joe — this is your Disneyland."

Rahm was beaming now, gazing lazily out the window as we rolled past block after block of shipping containers waiting to be loaded onto new boxcars.

"The size of the rail yard is something else, I'll give you that," I admitted.

"Sometimes, size *does* matter, Joe."

At that I managed a slight guffaw. A very slight guffaw.

Rahm received a call, and he excused himself from our one-sided conversation. He rolled up the tinted glass divider between the front and back seats. It was soundproof. I could guess what his end of the call sounded like, though. *Eff this* and *eff that.* Words I generally saved for big occasions and hot mics.

I caught Polaski staring at me. His presence was making me uncomfortable. He had a nickname — "Bento Box" — that I'd thought was a joke. Now, I wasn't so sure. The rumor was that his nickname didn't come from his love of sushi, but from his unique skill set: he could twist an opponent so out of shape that they would fit into a Japanese bento box.

"How much longer are we going to be driving around?" I asked. I should have had an ice pick — not only to break the ice between us, but for self-defense.

"Your flight doesn't leave until nine. You got someplace else to be?"

Bento Box had clearly progressed from bodyguarding politicians to doing their dirty work. He knew my schedule. It wasn't a leap to imagine he'd been tailing me from the moment he'd gotten wind I was in the Windy City. I'd been a fool to assume I could swing through town without the mayor's office knowing about it.

How much did Rahm know about what his fixer was doing behind his back? It seemed a little too convenient that he'd gotten an important call just as he'd picked me up. If I kicked out the divider between us, would I catch him listening in on Bento Box grilling me?

I decided to test the waters. "You were following me the whole time."

"I've been with the mayor all morning."

"I heard footsteps."

"This is a city of three million people. That's a lot of feet."

"So you didn't have somebody trailing me?"

Bento Box looked out the window. "If we did, it was for your benefit. You don't know this city. You don't know these neighborhoods."

"I'm a bad tourist."

"You want to be the next body, Joe?" Bento Box shook his head. "C'mon. You're smarter than that."

"My mama didn't raise no dummy."

He snorted. "Could have surprised me. I heard you were pretending to be an FBI agent. *Really?* I thought. *Is that true? No way Joe Biden could be that stupid.*"

I could feel my heart speeding up, my blood pressure creeping into territory my doctor didn't like to see. But my doctor wasn't here now.

Through clenched teeth I said, "If you want to know what I'm doing here, you could at least ask without badmouthing my mother. All I told that cop was that I was with the federal government. If she assumed I meant the FBI, that's on her, not me."

"You *used* to be with the federal government," Bento Box said. "Right now you've got about as much power in Washington as a garbage collector."

"An honest profession," I said. "Unlike some."

The fixer rolled his eyes. "You were in the Senate for almost four decades. Your record isn't spotless." He showed me a photo on his phone. "You ever seen this kid before?"

A mugshot. Shaun Denton was younger, with bloodshot eyes and that same sheepish grin I'd seen before. I tried not to think about him on that gurney.

"Don't know him."

"This is the thug that got popped back there," Bento Box said. "Deshaun Denton. Age sixteen. His record reads like video-game stats. Half a dozen arrests for petty theft. Four arrests for grand theft auto. Assault with an aggravated weapon — a charge dropped when the victim wouldn't testify."

I lowered my head. He couldn't have been talking about the young man I'd met today. There had to be a mix-up.

Bento Box continued, "He told the cops he didn't see who shot him, you believe that? If he's lucky, he'll die on the way to the hospital. If you don't bleed out from an injury like that, you could go into septic shock. Nobody wants to go through that."

I noticed we were on a freeway now. The driver had slapped a red emergency light on the roof. Cars were pulling over to let us pass. Where were they taking me? More important, what did they intend to do with me once we got there?

Everyone knew about the Rahmfather sending a dead fish in the mail to a pollster. That was one way to send a message. His fixer surely had other ways of getting through to people. Bento Box scooted closer. He was so wide that he took up two full seats. "I'm going to give you one chance here, Joe. Tell me the truth."

"I —"

"And think about it before you answer. Think about it real hard. I'm not sure what kind of game you're playing, but I'll find out. I don't buy the stuff about trains. Rahm might, but I don't."

"I'm not sure what you want me to say."

"Tell me what you were doing in Englewood. What you were really doing."

The decorated ivory handle of a pistol was poking out of a holster inside his jacket. It would have been so easy to tell him the truth. To tell him that I thought Shaun had stolen Barack's BlackBerry, and that I had taken it upon myself to give the kid a stern talking-to, and dang it, I was in over my head. But first I had to talk things over with Barack. This was his town, not mine.

Bento Box put an arm around my shoulders. "We can do this the easy way, or we can do this the hard way."

My only chance to escape was to try the door. We were on a freeway, but only going fifteen or twenty miles an hour due to the traffic. Survivable, as long as I didn't land on my noggin and split it open like an egg.

Joe Biden: sunny-side up.

I didn't like the sound of that. I didn't like it at all.

Before Bento Box could go to work on me, the window partition rolled down. The big man scooted back in his seat, as if he hadn't been crowding me the entire time.

Not that he'd said what would happen if I didn't tell him the truth. When you were the size of a grain-fed bull, you didn't need to be explicit with your threats.

"Sorry about that," Rahm said. Whether he was talking about the phone call or the unpleasant business with Bento Box, he didn't clarify. "Listen, Joe. I meant what I said about us. You and I. Let's start over. Let bygones be bygones and all that. You're going to need a friend in this town."

"I've got one."

"Barry isn't around much these days. You may have noticed, he isn't exactly the most popular guy in town anymore."

"They think he left them, that he forgot about them."

"They don't think that — they know it. And they don't want this, this library —"

"Community center."

"— this *community center* he's proposed in Hyde Park. You know what's going to happen to rent? To property taxes? To parking? The people are tired of it. They're tired of the millionaires, the billionaires. They're tired of the one percent picking winners and losers."

"You're part of the one percent."

"They hate me more than anyone."

"You won a second term."

"Chicago, baby," he said, without the slightest hint of irony.

"You want something from me."

"If a former vice president catches a lead shower in my city, the Feds really *are* going to step in. And once they set up camp, they're not going to leave. You've seen it."

He was talking about the race riots that had torn Wilmington apart in the wake of Martin Luther King Jr.'s assassination. The city was in flames. The country was in flames. The National Guard was mobilized to keep the peace where the local law couldn't handle it, which was pretty much everywhere. Within a month, calm returned to much of the country. In Wilmington, however, the Guard camped out for a full nine months.

"What are you asking me for?"

He handed me his business card. "I'm asking for you to trust me. That's it. If you run into trouble — if you need *anything* in this town — give me a call. This is my private line."

I started to say something but bit my tongue. Mirror-windowed buildings towered around us. We were back in the Loop, in time for Rahm to bully his way to the front of the parade. The driver cut through traffic like a hot knife through butter. We pulled up to the entrance to Navy Pier, Chicago's flashy tourist mecca on the lake.

I stepped out without saying goodbye. The pier was practically deserted, what with the parade about to begin any moment farther downtown. There were traces of the morning's crowds everywhere: a puddle of green beer here, a shamrock necklace there. Any other day, I would have loved to take advantage of the calm in the storm to ride on the pier's iconic Ferris wheel, which I'd eyed this morning on our way into town. It was a tourist trap, but dang if I didn't love me a good tourist trap.

I wasn't in a touristy mood right now.

Bento Box held out a fist. If he was waiting for a fist bump, he was going to have to keep waiting. But he wasn't looking to bury the hatchet. He was holding what was left of my sunglasses. "I think you dropped these," he said with a knowing nod.

"Not mine," I said, reaching inside my jacket and pulling out my backup pair. Ray-Ban aviators were among the top-selling sunglasses in America. A modern classic, as ubiquitous as AR-15s. He'd have to dust for prints if he wanted to connect them to me — not worth the time and trouble.

The smirk on his face slid off like he was melting in the high-noon sun. The SUV limo pulled back into traffic, leaving me in a cloud of exhaust. I could feel Chicago in my pores. It was going to take a good long shower to wash her off me, but there was no time to shower. I held up a hand for a taxi.

9

The Obamas' Chicago home was in Hyde Park. I knew approximately where the house was — not the address, but the nearest cross streets. All you needed to know was the general location. The Secret Service would let you know when you were getting hot.

The agent stationed on the perimeter of their block nodded as I passed. I rang the doorbell and took a step back. In all the years I'd known the Obamas, I'd never set foot inside their Hyde Park residence. It was their home away from Washington, a little respite from DC and its insular political scene. Whether I liked it or not, a part of Barack would always associate me with the swamp. No matter how close we'd grown, I wasn't part of his inner circle of friends from back in the day, the guys he used to shoot hoops with. He was a man who drew boundaries, and I didn't belong in this part of his life.

I was about to cross that boundary now.

"Oh!" A middle-aged Indian woman answered the door. Her eyes traced me from head to toe and back again. "Mr. Vice President."

"You can call me Joe," I said with a grin. Over the years, I'd become aware that I had a particular effect on women of a certain age. (Eighteen to ninety-one, in case you're wondering.) "Is President Obama home?"

"Oh, yes," she said, ushering me inside. Then: "Shoes off, please. Their rule, not mine."

I bent down and undid my laces. A twinge of pain shot through my lower back. I'd never had back problems, but the endless parade of airplane seats was getting to me.

"The president said you might be dropping by," she said.

"He did?" This was news to me. I'd gone back to the Tribune Tower to look for Barack, but the Secret Service told me he'd gone home for the day and wasn't scheduled to return for several hours. "I'm sorry, I didn't catch your name."

"Suleikha," she said, shaking my hand.

"You're their . . . housekeeper?"

"Live-in house sitter. Their housekeeper only comes on Mondays, Wednesdays, and Fridays." She paused. "And every other

Sunday."

"Must be nice," I muttered. I'd had a housekeeper at the VP residence. Now that I was out of office, Jill kept threatening to hire somebody to tidy up our home if I didn't pick up after myself. We had a house-cleaner who stopped in at our vacation home once every two weeks, but that was different. At least that's what I told myself.

Suleikha led me to the back porch. I don't know what I'd been expecting, but the house was as ordinary as a loaf of white bread. Their Washington house had come fully furnished. It was a sight to behold — a house staged by a realtor. This house had more of a lived-in feel. The beige shag carpeting was worn down by the years, and the walls were in need of repainting. The framed photos were all pre-2009, from the last time the Obamas lived here full time.

We stepped out onto the back porch. Barack was shooting hoops in the driveway. He shielded his eyes to get a look at his visitor and waved me down when he recognized me. No shock on his face.

He wiped sweat from his brow but turned and shot another basket. The ball bounced off the backboard and ricocheted down the alley.

"You want to get that?" Barack asked the

Service agent standing on the edge of the court. The agent darted after the ball like a dog for a Frisbee. Unlike Steve, this guy could take a hint when he wasn't wanted.

"I went looking for your BlackBerry," I said once the guy was out of earshot.

Barack raised an eyebrow. It was too deliberate to be a natural reaction.

"Didn't find the phone. I've got a lead on the thief, though."

"Shaun Denton," he said.

"Rahm talked to you."

He shook his head. "Shaun was volunteering at the conference. Michelle brought him into the green room to meet me. We shook hands, that was it; I was busy going over my notes for the keynote introduction. Later on, when I saw where my phone was, I put two and two together. I remembered reading his application when it came through the center and thinking the freight yard was an awfully grown-up job for a kid that age."

"When I was sixteen, I was slinging papers at doorsteps from my bike."

Barack didn't say what he was doing at sixteen.

"You suspected him," I said. "Why didn't you go after him?"

"I don't think he knew whose phone he'd taken. I'd left it on a table, he had sticky

71

fingers. Compared to everything else the kid had been through, if I'm remembering correctly, boosting a phone wouldn't even rate. What did he say when you confronted him?"

"I didn't get the chance," I said. "He'd been shot."

This time Barack's look of surprise was genuine.

The agent returned, bouncing the basketball, out of breath. He looked back and forth from Barack to me. "I'll wait on the porch," he said, setting the ball down.

I caught Barack up on everything I'd learned about the shooting. He listened, his face a stone mask. His jaw was clenched. When I finished, he asked, "What did the police say when you told them about the BlackBerry?"

"Nothing."

He squinted in the sun. "Nothing?"

"I didn't mention it to them," I said. "Guess I forgot. Now, before you go and tell me why that wasn't smart of me —"

"That wasn't smart of you."

"— let me explain. I wasn't sure if you wanted me to drop your name into the middle of this business. Whoever has your phone either shot Shaun Denton or was a witness. Either way, that places the thief in the green room at some point this morning. Do you really want the police to descend on the Tribune Tower and start interviewing people? What's it going to look like if your conference guests get dragged down to the station to give statements because the president's phone is missing?"

"It's not about my phone anymore. Somebody was shot."

"True, but can you imagine the blowback? Not only on the building security, but for the Secret Service. For our dear friend Steve."

"I don't believe this happened because of a lapse in security," Barack said.

"I don't believe so, either. All we have to do is compile a list of every person who was in the green room this morning before your phone went missing —"

"You're suggesting we do this on our own, without involving the police."

"That's what I'm suggesting."

"Just wanted to be clear. Continue."

"Nobody's a bigger believer in the boys in blue than Joe Biden," I said. This was my standard speech — Barack had heard it before, but it bore repeating, if only so that I could remind myself who I was. "Nobody's a bigger supporter of the men and women in uniform. But I also can't ignore the facts, which is that they've got their hands full today. Not only is it St. Paddy's weekend, it's also the first nice weekend of the year. The snakes are going to be out in full force."

"Snakes?"

"Criminals. Bad guys. Mobsters."

"Did Rahm tell you this? He could have been trying to scare you away from Englewood. Which would have been well within his rights to do."

I shook my head. "A bluebird could have told me, for all it matters. It wouldn't make it any less true. Besides, you should have been there — if you could have heard how the cops on the scene were talking about this thing. Like it was just another gang shooting. I met the kid. You did, too. He was no gang member."

"You can't tell by looking at someone if they're in a gang, Joe."

"But —"

"Forget whatever you've seen on *Law and Order.*"

He was right, but I continued my pitch. I was on a roll like honey drizzle. "We're the only ones who can do anything about this. You've got the connections, I've got the —"

"Aviators?" he said, taking a shot at me and the hoop in one graceful motion.

"The street smarts."

"Hmmmmm."

"I've got the drive, then. The fortitude. The resolve to see that justice is served. I've been a faithful cog in the machine my entire career. I did everything I was supposed to do. And then you came along and showed me how shortsighted I'd been."

"Joe —"

"Hold up, I'm not finished." I paused. "What were you going to say?"

"I was going to say that you're not giving yourself enough credit. The machine needs cogs. It doesn't work without them. The people of this country need good men and women like you in government. That said, I'm not sure this is the way to go. I suggest you call the mayor's office, get Rahm Emanuel on the horn, and say, 'Oh, wait, you know what, I do know that guy. I was having a senior moment.' Tell him about the BlackBerry."

I grunted a reply.

"No need to be like that, Joe. Rahm's a good guy," Barack said, shooting a solid three-pointer. "A little rough around the edges —"

"Like a serrated knife."

"— but he gets the job done."

I didn't have a reply to that, so I kept my mouth shut. It was as close to a compliment

75

as I would ever pay any of Barack's Chicago buds.

He dribbled the ball some more, but his enthusiasm for shooting hoops had waned. "Weren't you going to hang out at the airport on standby for an earlier flight?"

"Still haven't found the right souvenir for Jill. Might take all day."

Barack passed me the ball. I wasn't ready for it but caught it just the same. Some things you never forget. "Let's find your kicks."

And that was it. That was all he had to say for me to know we were on the same page. Brothers again — once and for always.

A cool gust hit me, causing a chill to run up my spine.

We both knew what we were getting into. We knew the risks, which we didn't discuss. There are some things in life worth taking risks for. Justice is one of them. With the police otherwise tied up, there was an opening for us to step in and lend a hand — off the record, of course. With Barack Obama's connections inside government intelligence agencies, we might even have had access to more information than the cops on the ground. Not that I expected him to use them. He knew I liked to play things above the board.

I could hear exactly what Jill would say if she knew what Barack and I were about to do: *You don't have to prove anything to anyone. You've proven yourself enough.*

This wasn't about other people. It wasn't about impressing anyone, except maybe the voices in my head — Ma and Pa Biden, and the lessons they'd imparted on me. It was about doing the right thing. As if that had ever been in doubt.

10

The task should have been easy: Find Barack's BlackBerry, find the shooter. Unfortunately, whoever had the phone had either drained the battery or turned it off. The trail was a dead end. Thankfully, that wasn't our only angle to work. A couple of phone calls to South Side hospitals was all it took to find Shaun at St. Bernard. He was out of surgery. Shaun had told the first responders he hadn't seen the shooter, but that didn't mean he didn't have suspects in mind. Barack didn't argue. He'd skimmed Shaun's social media profiles and come up empty. The only question was whether Shaun would be in any shape to talk.

I was done with public transportation for the day. Barack suggested we take his electric car, which the house sitter used to run errands. I'd seen it sitting out back, off to the side of the driveway. In fact, I'd mistaken it at first for a kids' Big Wheel. I didn't catch the make or model, because electric cars aren't cars. They're abominations.

"I'm not going to drive a car that you have to plug in first. I use a gas lawnmower and a gas string trimmer, and you better believe I'm going to drive a car that drinks gas like it's going out of style."

"It is going out of style, Joe."

I asked Steve, who'd reluctantly agreed to escort us, if he had a car in town. Usually, the Secret Service rolled around in these big, fat Suburbans that could chew up a lawn like nobody's business. Steve had something better: a sleek black 1980 Firebird Trans Am, rented from a collectible car rental agency. He was planning to visit his folks in Iowa after the Obamas left town. A little spring vacation. That was A-OK by me. I'd make sure the car was still in one piece when I was finished with it.

"I'm the only driver authorized on the rental agreement," he said.

"Those things aren't worth the paper they're printed on," I told him. "I went to law school, so I should know."

With me behind the wheel, we hopped onto the Dan Ryan expressway. The Firebird's T-top panels were off and the side windows were down, allowing the wind to whip my white hair to and fro. There was less and less of it every year, but it was still a full head compared to the tangled weeds some guys my age called hair. The radio was tuned to a classic rock station and cranked up. Steppenwolf blasting from the speakers. Not something I'd normally listen to, but the car demanded a little heavy-metal thunder: the turbocharged V8 engine had some real kick to it, like my brother-in-law's homemade honey mustard. Maybe that no-talent writer had been on to something when he'd put me behind the wheel of a Firebird in his book.

Steve was in the copilot's seat clenching his jaw. Barack was crammed into the backseat, his bony knees scrunched up to his chin like a gargoyle. A very uncomfortable gargoyle.

It was too bad he had to ride in back, not in the passenger seat, buckled in and ready for action. But Barack Obama was no ordinary passenger. The windows weren't tinted, and passers-by would spot him like a great white in a goldfish bowl. I didn't envy Barack's desire to be one of the regular people again, to pretend like he didn't have Secret Service surrounding him twenty-four hours a day. But there was nothing regular about Barack Obama, besides his bowel movements. And even then, who could be sure?

Traffic was moving faster on the Dan Ryan than on the city streets. All it cost me was six bucks. Actually, Steve would be picking up the tab. I was blasting through the toll stations and letting the cameras pick up his license plate.

The unmarked cop car tailing us was free.

The leprechaun was behind the wheel. Same fella with the red beard and green jacket I'd seen uptown. My first thought was that my eyes were playing tricks on me, but Steve saw him, too. Barack tried to turn his head, but he couldn't quite manage, all cramped into the backseat. He thought I was being paranoid. There were plenty of people dressed as leprechauns out and about today, he said.

And maybe I was a little paranoid. If so, it was for good reason. There was a saying I'd picked up from a bumper sticker years ago: *Just because you're paranoid doesn't mean they're not after you.* Bento Box had someone tracking my movements earlier in the day. I'd assumed he called them off.

I'd assumed wrong.

"That lane open?" I said, angling the rearview mirror so I could see better. The Firebird's power rumbled through my fingertips on the steering wheel.

Steve glanced around. "That's the shoulder —"

Too late. I'd already whipped out of traffic. Ahead, the shoulder was clear all the way to the next exit. I gunned it, kicking up gravel. Steve braced himself against the dashboard. Thing was, there wasn't anything for him to worry about. One of my nicknames may have been Amtrak Joe, but I'd spent more time behind the wheel than Mario Andretti. "Car Joe" didn't quite have the same ring to it, however.

I hit the off-ramp doing fifty-five and we bottomed out, sparks flying out from under us. The unmarked cop car followed suit. The light at the top of the exit was yellow. I had five milliseconds to decide whether to go for it or hit the brakes and pray they'd been serviced within the past decade.

I chose Option B.

The brakes locked up on me, and the sweet smell of burnt rubber flooded my nostrils. It had been a good long time since I'd smelled that delicious scent. The light turned red, and traffic started up in opposite directions. We skidded to a stop right before the intersection. Maybe an inch into it, if I'm being honest.

Steve had gone white as my knuckles. Life

gave him the heebie-jeebies. I'd never quite understood why someone so jumpy had gone into the Secret Service, one of the most stressful jobs on the planet. Like me, he probably liked a good challenge.

I tossed my phone to Barack.

"Check the map and see what route is the quickest from here to the hospital. Hurry before this light turns green."

Barack made a face in the mirror. "It says the fastest way is the Dan Ryan."

The light turned green.

"Did you hear me, Joe?" Barack said.

The leprechaun was idling behind us. Not honking. Waiting.

The light turned yellow.

"Let's see what this guy has under his hood," I said, pressing the gas pedal to the mat once the light turned red. It was drive-it-like-you-stole-it time. I'd never stolen anything in my life, but I had a lead foot heavier than Barack's summer reading list.

We shot through the intersection and merged back onto the expressway faster than you could say Jack Robinson. In the rearview, I spied the car that had been trailing us trapped at the stoplight by cross traffic. I didn't know why Bento Box hadn't called his man off. I was beginning to think his interest in keeping tabs on me and

Barack had less to do with our safety and more to do with keeping the city safe from us.

11

I thought there'd be some sort of police presence outside the boy's room on the third floor, but there was none. He wasn't even registered as a John Doe — he was under his own name. Whoever had tried to off him was free to waltz in and finish the job. I would have to ask Barack to hire some private security for the floor. No one had taken a second look at me in the halls. If I'd known things were so lax around here, I wouldn't have told Barack and Steve to wait in the car.

Shaun was laid up in bed, an assortment of cables and monitors beeping and whirring away. His eyes were closed. The black man in the fedora who'd nearly run me down outside the Tribune Tower was at the foot of the bed, a Bible in his hands.

He didn't look up at me as I entered. "He's a good boy."

"I'm sorry," I said. I glanced at Shaun and

felt my heart in my shoes. I'd stood by too many kids in hospital beds in my time. Way too many. I met the eyes of the man who'd spoken.

"Pastor Jenkins Brown," he said. "The Red Door. We're nondenominational."

"Joe Biden. Uh, Catholic."

"Barry's friend."

If he recognized me from outside the conference this morning, he didn't show it.

"Sorry I missed your breakfast earlier today," I said. "Traffic was awful."

"So was the catering. I cut out right after for some chicken and waffles from Harold's."

I laughed nervously. Shaun was sedated, according to the nurse I'd spoke to. Not in a coma. Just soundly asleep. He'd made it through surgery like a trooper. It was a miracle that the bullets hadn't hit anything important. Why didn't it feel like a miracle, then?

"Shaun went to your church, didn't he?"

"He's one of my kids. I've said that about all the children in our congregation, but Shaun is special. His mother passed a few years ago. A stray bullet. No father around, so our Holy Father stepped in."

"No other family?"

"An aunt. Selling herself on the streets.

Always drunk and high."

I shook my head. Pastor Brown spoke plainly about such matters, as if it was normal for a kid to lose everyone in his life before the age of sixteen. It wasn't normal. But, as I'd come to understand, the only strategy for coping with the abnormal was to accept it. To let it become one with you. Otherwise you could lose your mind.

"I also understand he got himself into some legal trouble," I said.

"Like most of the kids round here without any positive role models, he was caught up with the wrong crowd. Made some mistakes. I don't know what you heard, but all that was a long time ago."

"You said 'the wrong crowd.' Like a gang?"

"We got all sorts of gangs running the streets in the neighborhood. The Gangster Disciples, the BPS. The Crooks. They're all the same — selling drugs, jacking suckers. You can't live here without knowing someone in a gang. Was he ever a member himself?" He shrugged. "He's a member of the Red Door now."

"Would they have come for him?" I asked. "Maybe he made it out of the lifestyle but they weren't willing to let him go." It happened all the time in mafia movies, though I kept that tidbit to myself.

"The gangs know not to mess with one of my kids. Don't want to start a holy war."

"I've never met a criminal who had much respect for the word of God. As you surely know, when you break the law, you're probably breaking a commandment, too."

"They respect my word." He was squeezing the bed rail tight, causing it to tremble ever so slightly. He was angry, but he had a right to be.

"Shaun hadn't been in trouble for two or three years. He wasn't on probation no more. He found God. Or, rather, God found him. They had a strong connection." He paused. "They *have* a strong connection. They're not ready to meet yet."

I didn't say anything because there wasn't anything to say. Nobody — not Pastor Brown, not the Vatican — had the inside scoop on when somebody's number would be called. All I knew for certain was that every one of us on God's green earth was marching toward the end, closer and closer to heaven every day. I couldn't do anything about that but maybe, just maybe, I could find out who did this to Shaun. I promised I'd take a train around the world and back for him if he were my kid. And a Biden keeps his promises.

12

I returned to the Firebird. It was empty. Barack and Steve must have gone to stretch their legs. Standing there by myself in the parking garage, I could have been anybody. That would all change when I threw my ball cap into the ring for another run at the White House. The clock was ticking — not just on my age, but on getting a team together. Building support. I should have stuck around the forum, talked to Caruso. Was that what Oprah would have done?

What I needed was to get home. Recharge my batteries.

"Things don't look good, do they?"

I turned around. Barack was standing ten paces away, partly hidden behind a concrete beam. All I could make out was the outline of his dad jeans. I half-expected him to have a lit butt between the fingers of his left hand, but he'd quit years ago. If he picked up a cigarette, it meant that things had gone off the rails. With the direction the country was headed, I was surprised he wasn't chain-smoking.

"Shaun?" I said. "He's breathing on his own. Knocked out, but breathing. He's on a cocktail of antibiotics to ward off infection. They're going to keep him sedated at least overnight. He could go home as soon as Monday morning, though. He was lucky."

Barack stepped out of the shadows. "Steve has someone reviewing the security tapes at the Tribune Tower. There was no camera on the green room, or inside it, but there's plenty of video otherwise. They're focused on identifying anyone who may have been out of place. They're matching everyone on the tapes with the attendee log, to see if perhaps someone went down to the lower level who shouldn't have been there."

"That's going to take forever."

"Facial recognition software may speed things up a bit."

"I saw all the security in that building. I doubt they let somebody slip through who wasn't supposed to be there."

"We'll cross that bridge when we come to it."

He was too close to the situation to see what I could see. The Secret Service was looking for a needle in a haystack. They needed to start looking at the hay. The caterers and hotel staff. The conference attendees. The volunteer staff. The speakers. Barack's friends.

I'd let the Secret Service do things their way. For now.

"I don't suppose you have any contacts on the force?" I asked. "Anyone we can lean on to get our hands on the police report from the shooting?"

Barack shook his head. "They're loyal to the chief of police, who's loyal to the mayor. And from what you said, Rahm's in a fighting mood. Everybody owes somebody in this town. Trouble is, I don't have a lot of favors to call in."

"You didn't cut them enough pork when you were in office."

"I had an obligation to the American people, not just to Chicago. Even as a senator, I was always thinking about the big picture."

"All politics is local," I said, quoting the dearly departed Tip O'Neill.

"You were much better at the political stuff than I ever was, Joe."

I opened my mouth to argue, but he was right. I didn't want to step on his toes. Not when he was serving up humble pie.

"Ran into your pastor friend upstairs," I

91

said, switching to less fraught territory. "He didn't have much to say about Shaun, other than he was a good kid with a bad track record. Which we already knew, of course."

Barack nodded. He didn't correct me when I called Pastor Brown his friend. I'd assumed they were close.

"Didn't see any family upstairs," I said. "His mother's passed, his father's out of the picture."

Barack didn't say anything. Perhaps he knew this about the kid, perhaps not. He had written an entire memoir about his own MIA biological father. He knew the drill.

"He has an aunt," I said. "I assume she was — is — his legal guardian. He's only sixteen. She's not here, though, which is just damned odd. The pastor hinted she had some troubles of her own."

"She may not know what happened to him. You said yourself the police are over-whelmed today. Also, he could be crashing with a friend, if the aunt's house isn't safe."

An engine roared to life behind us. Its deep growl reverberated off the concrete, echoing throughout the garage like a minotaur stalking its prey in a maze. If I'd had a few more seconds, I might have been able to guess the make and model from its purr. I didn't have to guess. Tires screeched, and at that moment I saw the shock in Barack's eyes. Before I could turn around, he wrapped an arm around my waist and spun me out of the way.

Barack sidestepped the speeding BMW at the last possible second. The car spun out into the exit ramp, where it disappeared. We could hear the BMW making the rounds, tires squealing the whole way.

Steve, jumping out of the shadows, watched over the edge as the car went round and round. He turned back to us. "I got his plate. We'll have the police put out an APB and snag him. If he's drunk, they'll make an arrest. If not, I can send a couple of agents over to his house to give him a hard time."

"Beat him up?" I asked.

"Ask him questions. Tough questions."

I was breathing heavily. First the undercover cop on us, and now some fool in a Bimmer. I was tired of being chased for one day. It was time to do the chasing.

"What do you want to do, Joe?" Barack asked.

"That maniac almost killed us."

"You know how wound up you can get inside these parking garages. Don't tell me you've never stepped on the gas a little too hard rounding a corner and almost taken a few people out."

"I've never . . . OK, once or twice. But only once or twice. And never a president and former vice president. Almost took out a House rep once. Nobody important."

Now that the threat had passed, reality was starting to set back in. Did I really think chasing down some crazed driver was a good idea? It wouldn't have been my first car chase. But the last one had left Steve with a couple cracked ribs. So, fine, I said: let the Secret Service do their follow-up. We didn't have time for distractions. We didn't even have time for Shaun to wake up from sedation. The chances of bringing the shooter to justice were going down by the hour and would dwindle to next to nothing within forty-eight hours. Any idiot who'd ever seen a Dick Wolf produced television show could tell you that.

"Back to Shaun. If the shooting was workplace related, the cops would have been on top of that," I said, thinking aloud. "And if his friends were gangbangers, they're not going to come clean to us. No family to speak of. Who was working with him from your foundation? Did he have a mentor?"

"Caruso. Not sure where he disappeared to. I had Steve leave him a message to call us. He needs to know about Shaun."

I didn't like the sound of that. A kid is shot, and his supposed mentor goes off the grid. Still, nothing pointed in his direction. I had to be careful about jumping to conclusions. Especially about Barack's friends.

"The Rising Stars had to apply for the program, right? They must have put down contact information. An address. A next of kin."

"Michelle did all the processing."

"Then we'll get your wife on the horn —"

"She's with Oprah right now."

"I thought they were having brunch. It's almost one."

"And?"

"And that makes it lunch." I shook my head. "I don't care if Michelle is in a confessional with the pope. We need to get that paperwork."

"There's another way to get Shaun's paperwork," Barack announced in a take-charge voice that said we could change the world right now. It had been a long time since I'd heard him sound so certain, so confident. Together, we could solve this mystery. Bring the shooter to justice. Right a wrong. Some might have said we were wasting our time when there were bigger problems in America. In the world. But to me, there was no injustice too small to right

if I had the chance. And there was no one
I'd rather work with than Barack Obama.

13

"We can't just break into the building."

Barack was silent.

"Oh, no," I said. I should have slammed on the brakes right there, but we were almost to his foundation's temporary offices.

"Technically, it wouldn't be breaking and entering. As the foundation chair, I have every legal right to be in the offices. It's like breaking into your own car." The hitch was that he wouldn't be the one breaking in to pilfer the paperwork — I would. Through a secret tunnel from an adjoining building on the University of Chicago campus. The Obama offices were the only ones closed today. The rest of campus never locked its doors.

"You're pulling my leg," I said. "I can't believe you don't have a key."

"I was a professor at the law school for roughly a decade. There's a series of underground steam tunnels that connect every building on campus. They added security gates to the tunnel entrances several years ago, but when I toured our foundation offices, the gate wasn't padlocked."

"That's reassuring."

"There are sternly worded signs warning trespassers to stay out of the tunnels."

"And that keeps kids out. Sternly worded signs."

"When I was at the school, most kids were too busy partying to wonder what was behind the basement doors. The kids who did know about the tunnels were smart enough to heed the warning signs. The ceilings are low, and the walls are lined with massive steam pipes. Bump into one, and you would have wound up in the burn unit for the rest of the semester."

I looked at Steve, who was riding shotgun, to see if he found this as disturbing as I did. You couldn't tell what the heck he was thinking behind those pitch-black sunglasses of his. He might have been sleeping.

"You're sending me in by myself?" I asked Barack. "Why aren't you going in?"

"I'm going to provide a distraction."

"And how do you expect to do that?"

Barack grinned. "By being myself."

I pulled into a metered space in front of

the weathered brick building that housed Barack's nonprofit foundation. A couple of co-eds with backpacks walked past us on the otherwise deserted sidewalk — the rest of their classmates were either uptown at the parade or off-campus drinking themselves sick. Barack handed me his credit card to plug the meter.

"It's a holiday weekend," I said. "Parking is always free on holidays."

"Not in Chicago," he said.

I grumbled a few words that would have sounded more natural coming out of Rahm Emanuel's mouth.

"It's not even your credit card," Barack said. "I don't know what you're complaining about."

Thing was, I didn't know either.

As soon as I reached the steps of the building next door to the foundation's, Barack and Steve emerged from the Firebird. I watched from behind a row of bushes as Barack carefully rolled up his shirtsleeves, showing off his powerful forearms. He was unhurried, cool as a cucumber sandwich. The two girls stopped in their tracks.

This was Barack Obama. The man, the myth, the legend.

The distraction.

Barack introduced himself, though he needn't have been so modest. One girl held out her phone to take a selfie with him, almost as a reflex. Even though he had a strict no-selfies rule, today he was breaking it. He *wanted* to cause as much commotion as possible. In a matter of seconds, half a dozen students trickled outside. News traveled fast these days.

A bearded guy with a man-bun trudged down the stairs. He was on his phone. "Yeah, Barack Obama — the president. President Barack Obama!"

I slipped through the door. The last I saw of Barack, two dozen students were gathered around him. They seemed to be multiplying like rabbits. Hopefully, Steve could hold them off until I returned with Shaun's file.

I hurried down a long hallway, headed for the service elevator. It was empty. Following Barack's instructions, I took it down to the basement.

The elevator landed with a sharp thud. The doors creaked open. A kitchen. Normally, it would have been bustling with workers, but they'd all gone upstairs to get a glimpse of 44. I took a sharp left through a laundry room, where a dozen industrial washers were running, and then entered a storeroom marked FALLOUT SHELTER. It was one of those old yellow signs, the ones we'd plastered across the country in the fifties as we prepared for mutually assured destruction.

I flicked a light switch on the wall. A single bulb lit up. There were red-and-green tubs stacked all around. Three artificial Christmas trees leaned against the wall in a corner. I moved the trees aside, revealing a metal door with the warning sign Barack had told me about: POSITIVELY–NO–ADMITTANCE.

Had to admit, that was very sternly worded.

The door wasn't locked. The badly rusted knob turned easily — too easily. It fell off in my hand. This was not a good omen. Still, I was able to inch the door outward using my fingertips. It opened into a stairwell that led down to the tunnel.

The tunnel was lit with flickering emergency bulbs. *This is where democracy dies,* I thought. *In darkness.* Back at Archmere, me and the other academy boys had snuck through secret passageways similar to this. Without the hissing pipes that could land you in the ER. If I touched the wrong pipe, nobody aboveground would hear me scream. I'd once read that all it took was six feet of solid earth to soundproof a bunker.

Six feet was also the depth at which the dead were buried so that their rest would not be disturbed by the living.

I should have had a flashlight. Or at least a phone with a flashlight. The guy at the Verizon store had done me dirty, telling me that flip phones with limited functionality were about to "come back in a big way." I couldn't even get a signal down here.

I kicked something with my foot — a tipped-over plastic Solo cup, which rolled to a stop. A baby rat with big eyes poked its head out of the cup. He sniffed the air and blinked, dazed from being rattled around. He reminded me of the rubber rats Jill sometimes left on my podiums to scare the bejeesus out of me.

"Sorry to disturb you, little guy."

He blinked and retreated into his cup.

I heard the pitter-patter of little feet on the concrete behind me. *Scritch scratch, scritch scratch.* I swallowed hard. The little guy wasn't alone.

Terror rooted me in space. For the first time today, I began to wonder what the holy heck I was doing. OK, maybe not for the first time — maybe the thought had been running through my mind the entire time I'd been underground. Maybe it had been running through my mind since I'd bolted from the conference to hunt down the BlackBerry. All I knew was that I was seconds away from the rats chewing their way through me, suit first, skin second. Bones third. Whatever's inside bones fourth.

Barack had warned me of the hissing pipes along the walls. He hadn't mentioned the ravenous rats chock-a-block on keg beer.

I didn't know how much farther I had to go to reach the correct stairwell. I didn't know if my bum knee would pick now, of all times, to start acting up. All I knew was that if I didn't start pumping my getaway sticks, democracy wasn't the only thing that was going to die in the darkness.

So I ran.

14

The first stairwell I found opened into a musty basement that looked like every campaign field office I'd ever been in — a complete mess. I picked up a piece of paper on one of the desks. It was printed on Obama stationery. This was the right place. The Rising Hope Center. I wasn't getting eaten by rats. Not today.

I flipped on the lights. My heart skipped a beat when I saw Barack standing in the middle of the room, arms crossed and grinning. It wasn't him, however — it was a cardboard stand-up. I was all alone in the office.

A row of cabinet drawers lined the far wall. Beside them sat a foosball table, lending the space a vibe closer to a Silicon Valley company than a professional adult workplace. I knew a little about foosball tables: one night my aides had found one in the basement of the Eisenhower. Legend had it that the table once belonged to Jimmy Carter, a two-time regional foosball champion in Alabama. It was the kind of myth almost dumb enough to be true.

I never brought it up with Jimmy.

I rifled through the cabinet drawers looking for the application paperwork. There were folders and dividers, but most were packed tight with financial records. According to Barack, hard copies were the most secure way to store things in a world where anything digitized was fair game for hackers. Yet here I was, "hacking" the records using the oldest of old-school methods. The only way to prevent someone from stealing information was to not write it down in the first place. And even then, some enterprising criminal would eventually devise a way to hack your ideas directly from your brain. Human ingenuity knew no bounds, so long as there was enough money on the line.

I moved on to the next filing cabinet and hit the Powerball.

The applications — hundreds of them — were in alphabetical order. I flicked through until I found the Ds at the back of the drawer. *Darrow . . . Decker . . . Denton. Deshaun Denton.* Five pages. His legal guardian was identified as Chelyne Woodson. Relationship: aunt. There was an address and contact number.

Footsteps. Upstairs. A janitor? Or campus security?

I'd been planning on leaving through the front door — no sense risking the rats in the tunnel again. That plan was shot to heck. Even though I was within my rights to be in the offices, there was no telling how much time would be wasted if I was detained by security and forced to talk my way out of the building.

I pocketed Shaun's application. Doing double-time, I slipped back through the unsecured door and down the stairwell. There weren't any rats waiting for me. The second my feet hit the concrete, I took off in a sprint.

Five minutes later, I was still running. In retrospect, I should have paused on the stairwell to catch my breath before scampering off willy-nilly. It was clear what happened — I'd headed right instead of left, or left instead of right. Okay, not so clear. I backtracked through the tunnel. Ten minutes later, and I reached a fork. I hadn't remembered a fork. I was all sorts of turned around and mixed up six ways to Sunday.

I glanced over my shoulder. Was that heavy breathing I'd heard, or just the pipes? Shadows crept in around me. An amateur trespasser might have been frightened to the point of wetting his pants. Barack hadn't said the tunnels were haunted, but there was old history in this city. Dark history. The air went cold here and there in the tunnels. Random drafts. A phenomenon the less skeptical sometimes believed was evidence of paranormal activity. The university didn't need a ghost hunter; they needed a contractor.

After several minutes standing still, I decided no one was on my tail. Not this time. I veered left and continued until I reached another set of metal stairs. They all looked the same. I didn't care — I just wanted out. It seemed like I'd been pinging around all afternoon. When you get lost in space, you also get lost in time.

I opened the door and was greeted by a sheet of plywood. The back of a wooden bookcase. There were high-pitched giggles on the other side. Too young to be college kids.

". . . hopped together all around the garden. We hopped over daisies, we hopped over tiny carrots . . ."

A woman's voice, muffled.

There was barely enough space for my fingers to fit between the edge of the bookcase and the doorframe. I had to push it to the side carefully, without sending it toppling over, which could be trouble. If I dropped it on a bunch of kids, Biden 2020 would be over before it officially began. Heck, even I'd vote for Oprah over a guy who pushed bookcases onto children.

They say you're supposed to "lift with your legs, not your back." Fine advice. Not very practical. I never skipped leg day — once a month, I did a few kicks on those machines at the Y. You know, the ones where you lift the weights with your legs. I could do forty, fifty pounds. In the real world, though, you couldn't isolate your glutes or quads like that. You had to use what your mama gave you.

And what Ma Biden gave me were pencil-thin legs and a lower back made of iron.

The kids on the other side started shouting as the bookcase screeched along the tiled floor. By the time I moved it far enough to the side to squeeze through, I realized that I was interrupting story time. A dozen boys and girls, all around preschool age, were seated cross-legged on the floor. They were staring at me with wide eyes, like I was some sort of mole monster that had emerged from underground.

To my left was a terrified young woman with clear-framed specs, clutching a picture book like a shield. I recognized the cartoon bunny on the cover. Marlon Bundo. The miscreant who was dropping rabbit pellets on the carpet Jill had installed at One Observatory Circle.

Before I could apologize for interrupting, the woman swung the hardcover over her head and brought it down on my face. It wasn't enough to knock me out, but the shock of being thwacked caused me to stagger. That was all the opening she needed. She slugged the edge of the book into my gut like a battering ram. The air went out of my lungs, and I instinctively backpedaled to get away. The heel of my right shoe caught the lip of the doorframe and I tumbled backward, somersaulting down the staircase and into the darkness.

15

"Tell me again how you ended up inside 57th Street Books," Barack said. We were standing in line at Valois, a cafeteria-style diner that he used to frequent during his years in academia. I was lucky not to have broken my neck tumbling down the stairs. Once the bookseller realized who I was — one of the kids pointed and shouted that I was "the president's brother" — she helped me back up.

I explained all this once more to Barack, who still couldn't believe how I'd wound up over a quarter mile away from the foundation offices. He asked if I needed a bag of ice for my nose. It hurt like an accidental circumcision, but I didn't need ice. I needed to get my bearings, that was all. I could handle a little pain and swelling.

I grabbed a tray at the counter. There was a special "Obama Menu" tacked on the wall, underneath the regular menu. All of the president's old favorites were represented: eggs, bacon, wheat toast. Barack ate a little better these days — less grease, more fruit and veggies — but I wasn't going to be the one to issue a correction. There were a handful of OBAMA ATE HERE coffee mugs for sale. It was the first Barack Obama merchandise I'd seen in Chicago. At one point, there'd been an entire industry built around his image: T-shirts, dolls, action figures, buttons. Even pillowcases. (The pillowcases weirded me out a little, to be honest. I'd seen my fair share of unlicensed Joe Biden merchandise, but nobody had printed my face on a pillowcase. There were some lines you didn't cross. Drooling during the night on your favorite politician was one of them.)

As we made our way through the buffet line, Barack lowered the bill of his Cubs cap — or, more accurately, Steve's Cubs cap, which was on loan to the president. Steve was a diehard Cubs fan. Chicago's North Side team had long been lovable losers (which explained a lot about Steve). But then the Cubs won the 2016 World Series, ending the longest championship drought in professional sports history. It was a victory overshadowed by the election just days later. Suddenly, the Dems had taken over the mantle of "lovable losers."

Barack looked distinctly uncomfortable. Almost constipated. As a White Sox fan, it was the ultimate sacrilege to don the other team's logo. I told him it wasn't that bad. Delaware didn't even have a Major League sports team. We had to borrow Philadelphia's.

"I'd rather be wearing a Phillies cap," Barack grumbled. The Cubs hat paired well with the North Face windbreaker Steve had also loaned him. Barack looked like the saddest guy in witness protection.

"Not exactly what I expected," I said as we sat down.

"You don't like the food?" Barack asked.

My plate was stacked high with every breakfast item on the menu. "You're not really a fan of greasy spoons."

"Except when he's on the campaign trail," Steve said.

We both looked at Steve, who stuffed his mouth full of ham. He'd been on that caveman diet for so long that his eyebrows were beginning to grow together.

"I ate a little differently when I was younger," Barack admitted. He had a bowl of green beans and an herbal tea. That was it. It wasn't some cover, like he was trying to pretend he wasn't Barack Obama and not order the "Obama" off the menu — this was the *real* Obama, the one with gray hair, smile lines, and an AARP card.

I ate better when I was at home, but I wasn't at home. By midnight, I would be, if we could make some headway on this case.

It was a long time between now and midnight.

"So, the question is, what now?" Steve asked, chewing with his mouth open.

"Were you raised in a barn, boy?" I asked.

He kept chewing. "Just because I'm from Iowa doesn't mean I grew up on a farm. For your information, I was born in a hospital. Same hospital as Ashton Kutcher, in fact."

"That's impressive," Barack said, bringing the full weight of his sarcasm to the table.

Steve filled his mouth with another thick slice of ham.

"So, what now?" I said, repeating Steve's initial query. "I don't know exactly, but I'm not heading home with my tail between my legs." I paused. "And no, I don't have a lizard tail, to knock one of your other conspiracy theories off the shelf."

"I've seen you swim, sir," Steve said. "I'd know if you had a tail."

"Why are you still talking?" I asked.

I shouldn't have snapped at him. I was

frustrated. Everywhere we turned, we were running into brick walls. I'd never been able to get a feel for the city. I liked New York style pizza with thin crust; I liked my politics free of corruption. I didn't want to throw in the towel, but we weren't just up against criminals — we had a whole damned city to contend with. A city that didn't put ketchup on hot dogs.

A couple of hours into my day trip and already my outlook was blacker than Steve's coffee. In Chicago, there was a shooting every three hours. A murder a day. This weekend was shaking out to be its most violent in many months. That was why Rahm had blown me off. He didn't need me causing him headaches. Not this week-end. The city could erupt into flames at any moment. The police were mobilized to put out the fires before they spread, but they couldn't stop them from starting in the first place. The people were the matches. The city herself the kindling.

Steve's phone buzzed. As he took it out, the butt of his pistol peeked through his jacket. He listened without speaking. After he hung up, he said, "The lead on Shaun's aunt didn't exactly pan out. The phone listed for her is disconnected. The agent we sent over to her apartment said she wasn't home. She still hasn't shown up at the hospital."

Barack set down his cup of tea. "Do we know where she works?"

Steve shot him a disbelieving look. "Her nephew was almost murdered. You think she's at work?"

"This may come as a surprise to you, Steve, but not everyone has a job with paid vacation or sick leave. She may not have a choice: either go to work, or lose her job."

"Find another one if your boss is that much of a dick. I did."

We didn't need to ask Steve what boss he was referring to.

"Be that as it may," Barack said, "not everybody in this world has that sort of freedom. Is the jobless rate at an all-time low? Close to it. Are the jobs many Americans have worth a damn? We all know that answer."

I balled up my napkin. I wasn't finished with my plate, but I'd heard enough.

"We need to find out where this aunt works," I said, cutting off Barack's stump speech. There would be plenty of time to discuss America's broken paid-time-off system later. There wasn't a false note in the tune he was singing, but there was a time for talking and a time for action.

Be the change you wish to see in the world, Barack was often misquoted as having said.

When I picked up my tray, I quoted his wife instead: "Let's move."

16

Steve worked his contacts to pull together a dossier's worth of information on Shaun's aunt, working off what we'd found on the application. A cross-check with the IRS revealed her last known place of employment: a grocery store named Han's, on the western edge of Englewood.

In stark contrast to the blighted area around the freight yard, this section of the neighborhood was alive with activity. A group of jacketless young men here, a woman pushing a child in a stroller there. This wasn't the war zone the media and politicians made it out to be; it was a neighborhood. A neighborhood with problems, but also with people who lived and worked and socialized like in any other neighborhood in America.

I could feel eyes on us as we stepped out of the car, people watching from behind curtains and blinds. Barack, with his cap and windbreaker, was the only one of us that didn't look like a G-man.

Han's wasn't so much a grocery store as it was a convenience store. It was squeezed into three hundred square feet, smaller than my sunporch at the beach house. What food they did have on the shelves was mostly junk food. I'd read about "food deserts," poor neighborhoods without grocery stores. I hadn't realized some of the grocery stores were food deserts themselves. There was always the Whole Foods half a mile away. If you could afford to shop there.

A middle-aged black woman was working the register. Chelyne? I squinted. The nametag read "Chelly." Had to be her. She didn't appear to be the junkie that Pastor Brown made her out to be. Maybe I was holding onto my own outdated ideas of what drug users looked like. I'd been wrong about that sort of thing before.

I opened a refrigerated case and reached for a Dasani.

Barack poked his head over my shoulder. "Is that all they have?"

"It's water," I said. I peered at the label to see if I could tell where it had been bottled. Most of the time, you were getting some other state's tap water. This one said Oak Park, Illinois. "It's local."

"No Smartwater?" He looked up at Chelly. She was counting out change for a kid.

"That the one with electrolytes?" she asked without looking. She didn't smell like she'd been drinking or toking the reefer. She smelled like cookies 'n' cream hand lotion.

"That's the one," Barack said. "The distillation process replicates the hydrologic cycle to create water that's pure as rain."

"We don't have it."

Barack rolled his eyes behind his sunglasses. I didn't actually see him do it — the glasses were reflective for a reason — but I knew him well enough to know which way his eyes rolled.

Steve tossed a sugar-free energy drink onto the checkout roller alongside our waters. I waited to see if he was going to pony up. He made no move for his wallet.

I started to hand Chelly my credit card but she stopped me. "Cash only."

While I fished in my wallet, Barack spoke up. "Your nephew Shaun Denton?"

She didn't look up. "I already told y'all, I ain't seen him or heard from him in three weeks." She had a weary look on her face. We weren't the first strangers to visit her at work or knock on her door with bad news.

"We're not with the police," I said. "We're more like friends of a friend. We have some difficult news to share. If you have a few minutes —"

She shook her head. "I don't have a few minutes. Even if I did, I already heard what happened to him. He got his ass shot. I told him if he kept hanging around with that crew, something bad was going to happen. And it did."

There was no pity in her voice.

I wished I'd started our conversation differently, with a little small talk. But she'd known why we were there from the jingle of the bell on the door. Why else would a couple of white guys in suits be in here wasting her time?

"He has a part-time job," I said. "At the freight yard. Is he into trains?"

"You think I'm into cigarettes and Lotto tickets cuz I work here?"

"We're just trying to get a feel for the kid," I pleaded.

She counted my change back. "The only train he ever set foot on was the L. He sits in a booth at the yard and checks shipping containers in and out. It keeps him out of trouble a couple days a week. Or it did."

"He's part of a mentoring program for urban youth," I said. "He had so much going for him. I don't understand how this could happen."

"He meets with this rapper once a month at that center in Hyde Park. How's a rapper going to help him get through high school? What he needs is a tutor. Especially now, if he's out of school laid up at St. Bernard's for longer than a couple of days."

What he needed now was prayer.

Barack took a sip from his bottle, then looked at the label with satisfaction. As if he could taste how local it was. Chelly looked him over suspiciously. I worried that she'd recognized him, but we were saved by the door jingle. A pair of teenage girls came in, and she turned her attention to them. We were yesterday's news.

I tapped Barack on the arm. "Let's go," I hissed.

Barack started to follow me, then paused.

"You mentioned a gang," he said.

Chelly whipped her head around. "A gang?"

He nodded. "You said Shaun was hanging around with a gang. Do you know its name? We're trying to build a list of his known associates. We're trying to find out who did this to him."

"I never said gang," she clarified. "I said

crew. And the crew that he rolls with call themselves the Red Door."

17

On one of our visits to Chicago in 2008, Barack had given me a short history lesson on why the city was still so racially segregated, despite it being such a liberal haven. African Americans had moved here from the South in the early twentieth century, during what came to be known as the Great Migration. They settled on the South Side, where jobs and housing were plentiful. Unfortunately, white Chicagoans were as resistant to integration as the Southerners they'd left behind. They threatened African Americans who tried to buy into their North Side neighborhoods. Refused to sell to them. Threw rocks through their windows when any did manage to break the color line. The usual bag of dirty tricks. Though progress toward equality had been made in the past century, structural racism meant that the city was still largely divided in two.

I was getting a firsthand education on the

legacy we'd handed down to our brothers and sisters on the South Side. It was much more visceral than sitting down with Caruso would have been. I'd seen poverty and its effects in Wilmington, but nothing on this scale. We were heading back to the car from Han's. Half the homes and businesses we passed were boarded up. There were disturbing yellow signs stapled on rotting telephone poles warning residents to STOP FEEDING THE RATS. WE NEED YOUR HELP TO ELIMINATE THE RODENT PROBLEM IN THIS AREA. Yet life went on, all around us.

"What was that stuff about the trains?" Barack asked me.

"Nothing important."

"Is that why you're so interested in finding this kid's shooter? Did you think he was a fellow railhead?"

"It's not like that," I said. "It's not like that at all."

It seemed like he wanted more from me, but we were cut off by the deep bass of a passing Cadillac DeVille. It was a freshly waxed beauty, and it rolled up to the curb beside us. Caruso was behind the wheel. He turned down the music.

"Y'all need a lift?" he shouted through the open passenger window.

Barack told him we were parked right

around the corner, but thanks. It seemed improbable that in a city of this size he would just happen to drive past us. This was in his neighborhood, though — and word must have gotten to him that we were around.

Barack introduced us. I leaned on the door and shook his hand. He had a strong grip.

"Heard some good things about you," I said.

"And some bad things, right?" he joked. "Sorry I had to run this morning. Had to put out a fire."

"Did you hear about Shaun?" Barack asked.

"Shaun? From the program? Tell me he didn't do some ignorant shit again."

"He's at St. Bernard's. He was shot. He's out of surgery —"

Caruso slapped his steering wheel and muttered a string of obscenities.

"You might be able to help us find the shooter," Barack said, filling him in on what we knew so far, which admittedly wasn't much. Barack didn't say a word about the Red Door.

Caruso was shaken by the news. He'd already passed sadness and was onto anger. "I'm sorry. I'm going to see him now. I'll see you tonight — we can talk more then."

We watched him spin the wheel and tear off down the street. Steve cleared his throat. The Secret Service didn't like it when their protectees lingered on sidewalks. A couple of kids ran past us, causing Steve to visibly tense up.

Barack turned to me. "Not how you planned on spending your Saturday, is it?"

"Remember what you said?" I asked him. "If there's a child on the South Side who can't read, it matters to you. Even if it's not your child. How did we let things get so bad?"

"Believe it or not, things have been getting better. If you think Chicago is violent today, you should have seen it a hundred years ago. Take one of those gangland tours sometime, see for yourself."

Steve cleared his throat again, louder this time.

We both turned to him.

"Sorry to interrupt," he said, "but it's 2:30, Mr. President."

Barack groaned.

"What's the matter?" I asked. "The Bulls playing?"

"I'm supposed to give a speech at the forum at three. I haven't even started writing it yet."

126

We loaded ourselves into the Firebird. Steve mapped the Tribune Tower's address on my phone. It showed us arriving there at 3:05, based on current traffic conditions. I liked a good challenge.

Steve reached for the radio, and I slapped his hand away.

"I just wanted to turn it up," he said, rubbing his wrist.

"Leave it alone," I spat. "You don't touch another man's radio." One of the many life lessons Pa Biden had drilled into us when I was a kid. If only the youth these days had someone to guide them in life, like I'd had.

It was an outdated way of looking at the world, and I knew it. Even if you had somebody in your life, there was no guarantee they would lead you down the straight and narrow.

Take Pastor Brown, for instance. Barack trusted him. I'd learned that they'd worked together back in Barack's community organizing days. Barack valued loyalty above all else. I had no reason to doubt that the pastor's motives were pure. The Red Door didn't sound any different from thousands of other churches that did good work in neighborhoods across the country. Plus I had no room to talk; the Catholic Church had its own troubles. When you point a finger at somebody, three point back at you. (The thumb kind of sticks to the side, pointing at nothing or no one in particular, but I'll let that slide.)

Shaun's aunt was convinced the pastor and his church were trouble. She didn't go into detail, though — her manager had come back from lunch and that was the end of our conversation. On our way out, I saw her bury her head in her hands.

Barack refused to believe his friend was involved in any way with the shooting. He did acknowledge that Pastor Brown's particular mission made some folks nervous. The pastor's forte was "rehabbing" wayward youth. Jenkins Brown had been through the legal system himself, having robbed a liquor store when he was younger. Now he helped kids who were on the same path get off the street. And he was successful at it — his kids stayed out of trouble, for the most part. But what if his church operated like a prison? Not in a literal sense, but in the sense that prisons had become places for criminals to pool their resources and knowledge. What if the kids Pastor Brown was helping were teaching each other how to pick locks and boost cars? They weren't staying out of trouble, in other words. They were just becoming better at not getting caught.

Of course, I couldn't bounce my theory off Barack. I couldn't accuse the pastor without evidence. I didn't even know what I would be accusing him of. Was it really possible for him to have pulled the trigger at the freight yard? He'd left the economic forum after the prayer breakfast. He'd been in a hurry, too. And not very happy about it.

Getting your hands dirty — really dirty — has a way of rubbing off on you. It's tough to get them clean again afterward, no matter how hard you scrub. Lady Macbeth knew it. You can wash the blood off, but it's never really gone.

18

I stood in the wings with Barack while he was introduced. I'd pulled up in front of the Tribune Tower with enough time for the president to get a shave and a haircut, but of course he took the free moments to meet with some young fans backstage.

The speaker introducing him went by the name of Erick Rothschild. Barack Obama didn't need an introduction, especially in front of a hometown crowd. Still, it was customary to have a warm-up act. Even Roy Orbison had one when I saw him at the Delaware State Fair in 1977. Tom Petty. A pretty good opening act, as far as opening acts go.

Rothschild was the billionaire CEO of Monteverde, an alternative energy company he started in his bedroom in the great state of Montana. At a time when the United States was backing out of international climate accords, it was a pleasant surprise to find enterprising young folk like Roth-schild taking the initiative to pave the way for a better, cleaner future.

He was no Tom Petty, though.

"— and now let me welcome to the stage, President Barack Obama!"

I clapped Barack on the back and told him to break a leg. Which is a strange thing to wish upon somebody, especially a dear friend. It was one of those sayings you don't really think about, like, "Go fly a kite." I might as well have told Barack to go fly a kite, for all the good it would have done. You couldn't hear a thing, the applause was so deafening.

The crowd's fervor carried Barack to the podium, but quickly died down. Some had seen his brief remarks that morning, before Caruso's keynote. The audience now was three times the size, though. Standing room only. There was a nervous energy in the air. Barack's return to his hometown — and to public life — had been slow. We'd both spent the first year out of office sitting on the sidelines, watching the news while sitting on our hands. It was like selling your house and seeing the buyer chop down every tree you'd planted.

"Chicago," Barack said. "How you doin'?"

The thunderous applause returned, and

Barack broke into a wide smile. "It's been a minute." The line garnered a few chuckles. Like my grandmother used to say: it was funny because it was true. The crowd relaxed.

Barack started with what sounded like a rehearsed ode to his adopted hometown. After his first couple of years as an undergrad in California, he'd picked up and moved to New York. He'd needed to get away from that carefree attitude out west — to get as far away from Hawaii as possible. He wanted to distance himself from his friends, his classmates, his family. Be a serious student. Take up law. He'd somehow convinced himself that he had to live like a monk in a studio in Harlem. To bear down and study. His mother and sister visited him during this time. "Why don't you *smile* anymore?" his sister Maya had asked.

In Chicago, he'd found his smile again.

In Chicago, he'd found himself again.

Sweet home Chicago.

Barack repeated a lot of the same points he'd hit during his rally appearances last fall. These days, he spoke less of hope and more of change. It was a call to action. Neither of us had a pool of speechwriters to help us prepare our remarks — that era was long gone. Our old speechwriters were all podcasting now. One of these days, I was going to have to ask someone what in blue blazes a "podcast" was.

Barack had told me to wait around for him after his speech, but I had no such intentions. I didn't want to get him into trouble with Rahm or anyone else in Chicago. This was his town, not mine, but sometimes it's hard to see the forest for the trees. The Red Door was a giant sequoia. I wasn't accusing Barack of covering for his friend — at least not consciously. But we all overlook our friends' flaws. That's how friendship works. Even when they look guilty to the world, we can turn a blind eye. I'd seen it a thousand times. I'd been guilty of it, too. If I was going to open Barack's eyes to the possibility the pastor wasn't all he was cracked up to be, I had to dig up some dirt.

19

If I took the Firebird, there was a good chance I could poke my nose around Pastor Brown's church and be back before Barack knew I'd even gone anywhere. The way he was feeding off the crowd, he'd be speaking for at least another hour. Maybe two.

Borrowing Steve's car wasn't going to be easy, since I'd given him back the keys. The second and more significant barrier was that the Firebird was being loaded onto a flatbed by a particularly unresponsive and unsympathetic tow-truck driver.

"Don't you know who I am?" I said. My voice was already hoarse from screaming at him.

"Yeah," the driver said. "You're a guy that's going to need four hundred bucks to get your car back from the towing yard."

It was my fault. Sort of. When I'd dropped Barack and Steve off at the Tribune Tower, I was supposed to sit in the car, idling, until a Secret Service agent could be dispatched to park it for us. I'd seen no point to that, since there was a perfectly good parking spot less than half a block away on Michigan Avenue. I wasn't about to give up such a *primo* location, so I'd given the Firebird some gas and whipped around the corner and into the spot before anyone could steal it from me. I'd jumped out and checked the meter and saw a red flyer attached to it. Parking was restricted until 4 p.m. due to the parade. However, people had been streaming back to their cars. I'd assumed the city wouldn't enforce the parking restrictions, since the parade was over.

Apparently, I'd been wrong.

I had thirty-seven bucks in my wallet, not counting a couple of coins in my pockets. Not enough to bribe the tow-truck driver with. Maybe in 1967. Not that the guy cared, but my sleek, brown leather wallet was worth more than the cash in it. It had been a gift from Barack our final week in office. It was stamped with the White House seal, with my initials in the corner. Coincidentally, I'd also gifted him a wallet — black suede, but also with the White House seal and his initials. I stared at the wallet in my hands and remembered that day, down to Barack's very words:

"This is like a good O. Henry story," he had said as he marveled at our matching gifts.

"O'Henry? An Irish writer?"

"American." Barack flipped open his wallet. "Oliver Henry. It was a pen name, so he might have been . . . Wait a second."

"Something the matter?"

He pointed at a photo of his kids that I'd inserted into the wallet. "Where'd you get the photos in here?"

"Oh, that's all Jill. She must have printed them off the Internet."

"Check yours."

I glanced inside and saw reproductions from Biden family photo albums.

"All Michelle's doing," Barack said.

I'm still not sure who started snickering first, but pretty soon we were both doubled over, hands on each other's shoulders, laughing up a storm. Each of us had farmed out the task of getting the other a going-away present. Jill and Michelle had conspired to coordinate the gifts. Only one photo in both wallets matched: a snapshot of Barack and me together at a basketball game, dressed down and leaning in to one another, sharing a chuckle.

"Need a lift?" a familiar voice said, breaking through my memories.

I snapped out of my daydream to see a black Suburban pulled up to the curb. The tow-truck driver was busy locking Steve's car down on the tow bed, not paying any attention to me. (I'd been flipping through my wallet — perhaps he'd sensed I didn't have the cash to bribe him. Perhaps he was an honest man in a city of thieves.) The SUV's rear passenger window was rolled down.

"Well?" Michelle Obama asked.

"I came out here to plug the meter," I said, returning my wallet to my jacket.

"That's your car?"

"A friend's."

"Your friend isn't going to be very happy," Michelle said. Either she didn't know the car was Steve's, or she was playing along.

She whispered something to the Secret Service agent in the driver's seat. Then she popped her head back out the window. "Don't worry about the car. I'll have someone take care of it. Why don't you hop on in? I'll give you a ride."

I had two options: I could keep up the lie that I'd only been plugging the meter, adding some bull honky about needing to get back to the conference for the end of Barack's speech. Or I could come clean and accept Michelle's invitation for a ride.

They say honesty is the best policy. In my experience, I had to agree.

Sometimes, however, you have to make an exception.

"See, the thing is, I have to get back . . ." I threw a look over my shoulder at the Tribune Tower right as Steve burst out the front door, sending the Van Heusen–clad security goon tumbling to the sidewalk. While they were tangled up on the ground, I scooched into the backseat.

"Where you headed?" Michelle asked. "The airport?"

Whether she knew it or not, she was giving me one last chance to change my mind. To put myself on standby and get back to Wilmington at a decent hour. No one would be able to fault me for leaving town early. Barack would understand. I'd been assaulted by a bookseller and chased around town by a leprechaun. When Shaun woke, he would understand. I didn't owe him anything — he would forgive me. I wasn't a real detective shelving his case. I was Joe Biden, former vice president.

If I gave up on finding him justice now, there was one person who wouldn't forgive me: Joe Biden.

"I'm headed to the Red Door," I said.

20

Even by Secret Service standards, Steve was in ridiculous physical shape. Jill had once shown me his Instagram account, which was filled with dozens of pictures of his "progress," a.k.a. shirtless selfies. I didn't know why anyone would want to see something like that.

Jill told me she didn't know, either.

No matter how finely honed a machine he had transformed his body into, Steve was no match for the horsepower under the hood of Michelle's Suburban. Through the tinted rear window, I watched as he became smaller and smaller.

Satisfied that we'd outrun him, I turned to Michelle. She'd been on her phone and hadn't seen Steve trying to chase us down. "Sorry, you were saying?"

"I asked if you were going to see the pastor," she said. "What time are you supposed to meet him?"

"I'm not meeting him. Just dropping by, since I missed him at breakfast."

"Do you want me to call him first? He might not be in."

"I was hoping to surprise him. If he's not there, I'll take some photos with his staff." I looked out over the dyed-green river. It was the color of the slime my grandkids played with. "You don't see that every day, do you?"

"Want to go for a swim, Joe?"

"Left my trunks at home."

"It's not as bad as it looks. The dye is nontoxic. The Chicago River isn't as polluted as it used to be. Every sewage pipe in the city once flowed right into it. This was a problem because the river drained into Lake Michigan, which is where the city's drinking water is pumped from. It took them a while to realize why people were getting sick and dying."

"So they stopped flushing their toilets into the river."

She shook her head. "They reversed the flow of the river."

"And where does it drain these days?"

"That's a good question," she said. "But I don't want to know the answer."

Neither did I. "Meant to ask, how was brunch?"

"It was all right. The eggs benedict —"

"Did she mention me?"

"You want to know if Oprah mentioned you."

I nodded enthusiastically, as if I'd been gifted a brand-new Pontiac G6.

"You're acting very strange, Joe. Even for you."

It took us driving past the address three times to realize that the Red Door wasn't a *church* church — at least not the kind I was used to. The Red Door's house of worship was a vast warehouse, all big and boxy like an old Best Buy. No steeples or stained-glass windows. No crosses. No sign with worship times.

There was a red door.

"That's got to be it," I said.

Michelle looked unsure, but GPS confirmed we were in the right place. "This used to be a bad area," she said.

"There are no bad areas — only bad people."

"Are you trying to mansplain the South Side of Chicago to me, Joe?"

I shut my yap.

They dropped me off at the curb right out front. There was a parking meter with a faded "out of order" label taped over the coin slot. Michelle wasn't staying. She had "other business to attend to" — and if it had to do with Oprah, she didn't say so. It was fine by me. The main reason I wanted her to go on her way was that Steve was bound to put out an APB with his Secret Service team: *Find Joe Biden.* I wanted them to be far away when the call came in. I didn't want to have to explain what I was up to before I could even get up to it.

Despite the fact that this had clearly been an industrial area at one point, the sidewalks were lined with tall, sturdy oaks. There were a few apartment buildings — new or remodeled, I couldn't tell — across from the church. A construction crew was working down the street on a lot, digging away at a pit. Gentrification in real time.

My phone rang. Jill.

"Hey, Honey Bunny," I said.

"Is now a good time?"

"Just cruising around with the former First Lady," I said, watching Michelle's Suburban turn the corner and disappear.

"Don't let me keep you, then. I was calling to let you know we might have some guests over for dinner tomorrow. The whole family. Everbody wants to see you."

"It's not a surprise party, is it?"

"Not anymore."

"Was this your idea?"

She laughed. "What do you think?"

142

My wife knew how much surprises made my skin crawl, and she loved watching me squirm. One time, aboard Air Force Two, she'd crawled into an overhead bin and screamed when I opened it. I had screamed, too.

She told me to have a safe flight home. "Save your appetite for tomorrow, though — I'm making your favorite."

"Ice cream?"

"Lasagna."

"That's Garfield's favorite."

"Tell me you haven't been feeding him pasta, Joe."

"Is that bad?" The orange tabby we'd adopted shared a name with the cartoon cat. It wouldn't have been my first choice for a pet name, but it was what his previous owner — an Amtrak engineer who'd passed away — had called him. "But for the record, you're saying I shouldn't feed him pasta? Is he on some sort of low-carb diet?"

Jill sighed. "We'll talk about it when you get home."

I told her I loved her. I tried to hide the exhaustion in my voice, but she knew I was running on fumes. Too many months on the road. What she didn't know was that I couldn't lay down and rest. This afternoon, I would be skipping my nap. A kid was in the hospital; that was enough to keep me going. A kid who'd all but said he wished he'd had a dad like me. Maybe this was my fight, maybe it wasn't, but I couldn't just stand by and do nothing, could I?

For the past year, my anger had been rising. The nationalistic rhetoric in our politics was out of control. Hate crimes were on the rise. I'd hit the StairMaster in every hotel gym from Poughkeepsie to Portland and hadn't shed a single pound of rage. For once, though, you could see some muscle definition on my upper body. Nothing like Steve, but enough that it was noticeable. Last time I'd seen Jill, she thought I looked too lean. Too gaunt. I told her I was getting down to my fighting weight.

21

The eponymous red door was locked. I pressed the doorbell enough times to annoy somebody into answering it. No one did. What if I was selling Girl Scout cookies? Their loss, I guess.

I peered through the tinted glass. I could see the lobby, carpeted and brightly lit. A couple of potted plants. A few framed paintings. A cross here and there. Wooden doors that must have led to the main chapel.

No reception desk or secretary. This wasn't the type of church that was open to strangers, the type that might offer refuge to lost souls seeking shelter from a storm. Then again, I wasn't lost and it wasn't storming. Time to check for another way in. It wouldn't bother me if Pastor Brown wasn't in. It would be better, in fact. I wanted to see the church with my own eyes, and not the church he wanted me to see. The truth I could see with my own eyes was the only truth I trusted these days.

"Truth" had somehow become subjective. Who had seen that coming? The country was crumbling in slow motion, dismantled and sold off under our noses. For people like Shaun's aunt, though — and for the residents of Chicago's poorer neighborhoods — things had been in disarray for a long time.

Half a block down the street, a moving truck pulled to a stop at a gated parking lot. The church's name was crudely stenciled on the side with spray paint. The gate drew to the side and the truck entered.

By the time I reached the gate, it had closed again. Rusted barbed wire atop the chain-link fence stretched around the lot.

The truck backed up to an open door. The loading dock. A good thirty yards from the gate. I could just make out a pair of guys unloading boxes from the truck. If the Red Door was involved in Shaun Denton's shooting, all sorts of criminal activity could conceivably be on the table. I'd come face-to-face with the opioid crisis last summer in Wilmington. What would I run into in Chicago? I had to get closer to see what was being unloaded.

Unfortunately, that wasn't going to happen at the present moment. Not unless I had the *huevos* to scale the fence and sprint toward the loading dock, all in full view of the workers and the camera on high. Something told me that anyone dumb enough to try that would wind up leaving their *huevos* dangling from the barbed wire like a pair of fuzzy dice from a rearview mirror.

I would have to get in touch with Barack sooner rather than later. I didn't want him worrying about me. If I waited too long, I would hear the whirring blades of a helicopter overhead, circling the South Side in search of an elderly man with white hair who had wandered into the "wrong" part of town on his own, like I was some escapee from an old folks' home.

I needed something solid, though. If I got on the horn with Barack right now, I was liable to spill my crackpot theory before it was ready for primetime. I'd never been what you would call a good liar. I was the kind of guy who shot from the hip. Who spoke what was on his mind. Barack would know if I tried to slip one past him. He was like Jill in that regard.

I had to ask myself why I was playing things so close to the chest. I'd seen the way Barack took the news that Shaun Denton had been shot. He'd bottled up his anger. Neither of us had known Shaun, not really, but Barack's feelings about gun violence were well documented. Right now, he was a ticking time bomb. What would happen if I let him know I suspected the pastor of wrongdoing? Would he recuse himself and ask that I step back and hand over what I had to the police? Would he give me the silent treatment? You'd have thought that after all the years we'd spent together, I would know what was going on between those big ears of his. Truth was, I had only the vaguest idea what he was thinking at any given moment. Meanwhile, I was an open book — what you see is what you get with Uncle Joe. For better or for worse.

We'd gotten nowhere asking questions and knocking on doors. It was time to change up our strategy. Or, rather, it was time to change up *my* strategy. Barack was out of the equation now. I was on my own. It was time to turn over some rocks and watch the snakes scatter.

22

I knew every snake den in DC, from the murkiest watering holes to the grandest five-star hotels. I knew which steak houses you were likely to run into Republican lawmakers, and which farmers markets the Dems frequented. But I wasn't in DC.

Furthermore, I didn't know who I was even looking for. A crooked alderman? A muckraking journalist? Somebody who could shed some light on the pastor and his operation. The trick was finding the right somebody. I knew one person in the city who could point me in the right direction. Whether or not he would help me, I didn't know.

I rang up the number on the card Rahm had given me. His private number.

After four rings, a recording kicked in. "Thank you for calling Chicago 3-1-1. If this is an emergency, please press 'one' to be transferred —"

So much for that.

An old yellow-and-black cab rolled past me with its light on. I half-expected another Ditka clone, but this cabbie was older, Middle Eastern. He rolled down the passenger window and asked where I was headed. Before I could answer that I hadn't the slightest idea, my phone rang.

It was Rahm. "Sorry about that. Screening my calls. Everything OK, Joe?"

"We need to talk. In person."

He gave me an address on Division Street. I got into the cab and handed the scrap of paper to the driver.

"The Russian baths," the man said with a knowing nod.

"A bathhouse?"

"Like a spa, with massages. But for men."

"How is it . . . for men?"

"They buck nekkid." He glanced at me in the rearview. "You still want to go?"

Although part of me thought Rahm might be pulling some sort of prank, I grunted an affirmation. If he wasn't there, I'd stick around for a massage. Sleeping in a different hotel bed every two or three nights had taken its toll on me. Even the most expensive luxury-hotel mattress in the world was no match for one in your home. The one with your bedside table. The one with your reading light.

The one with your wife.

I was dropped off in front of a two-story concrete building across the river. It was so utilitarian it might as well have been built in postwar Germany. In a city known for its architecture, you didn't expect to find such a hostile-looking structure, built more to withstand an aerial bombing than for aesthetics. There was no obvious signage with the name or hours. This was getting to be a frustrating trend.

Inside, the smell of hot coal was overpowering. The air, moist as a swamp. Fitting, since Chicago was built on swampland (unlike Washington, where the "swamp" had always been metaphorical). There were undertones of sweat, body odor, and gym socks as well.

A fair-skinned woman with a buzz cut greeted me. She was dressed all in white, like an orderly. "Can I help you?" she asked in a Russian accent so thick that I was sure she'd copied it from *The Bullwinkle Show.*

"I'm meeting someone," I said.

She passed a laminated rate card across the marble counter.

"Can I just poke my head in or . . ."

She tapped the card with one of her long fingernails. "Pay first."

I scanned the card quickly and pointed out the most economically priced service with the word "massage" in it. *Birch massage.*

I paid up, and she handed me a towel and a white felt cap. "For your hair," she said, as if caps were worn on elbows in Mother Russia. She slipped a red bracelet around my wrist, which I took to indicate the service I'd purchased, and pointed me in the direction of the locker room. To my surprise, there were separate men's and women's rooms. Perhaps it wouldn't be the nudist free-for-all that I'd been warned about.

I stashed my clothes into a locker and wrapped the towel around my waist. The cap was oddly shaped, like an upside-down tugboat. I left it behind.

The locker room exited into a small common area. Three wrinkled men were climbing out of a whirlpool, gabbing away. They were wearing the house caps, and nothing else. A masseur with hands the size of catcher's mitts was digging into a man's back on a towel-covered bed. Too wide to be Rahm. The masseur nodded at me, and I followed his eyes to the sauna, where I was apparently supposed to wait my turn.

When I opened the glass door, heat rolled out in great waves like smoke from a burning building. A dozen or so men in varying stages of undress were packed close together on a long, three-tiered cedar bench. Nobody was talking. Rahm might have been among them, but I didn't look too closely. I'd already gotten my eyeful of man-flesh for the day.

I took the first empty spot on the bottom-most bench. To my immediate left, two dark feet dangled dangerously close to my head. They were attached to a pair of impossibly long, skinny legs that I would have recognized anywhere.

"You're not going to say hi?" Barack Obama asked.

23

Barack invited me to sit next to him on the upper tier, where it was so hot, I could feel my hair begin to sweat. Rahm, sitting on the other side of Barack, had a smirk on his face.

I started to back in beside them when Barack screamed, "Joe! Where's your towel?"

"I hung it up outside the room," I said.

"Go get it," he said.

I was turning to leave when I heard a sharp *SNAP!* It took a millisecond for the pain on my right butt cheek to register, but once it did, I yelped like a puppy chasing a mailman. Rahm was swinging a wet rolled-up towel with a sly smile.

"Very funny," I said, stomping out to grab my towel — not to cover myself, but for retribution should he snap his towel at me again. As I reached for the door, Rahm and Barack broke out in laughter that didn't die down until I'd returned.

"We have to quit running into each other like this," I said.

Barack cocked an eyebrow. He didn't know if I was addressing him or Rahm or both of them, and, frankly, neither did I. I was trying to break the ice. Easier said than done.

The Russian baths weren't anything special. Just another good ol' boys club. I'd never been a good ol' boy. I'd never had the time. I'd always had a family back in Delaware who I went home to every night on the Amtrak. That didn't leave a lot of time after work for closing down the bars on Capitol Hill with my colleagues. I'd never played the game. Yet I'd won — I'd won plenty.

Right now I was questioning what Barack's game was, and what he was doing here with Rahm. I'd come to kick over rocks. Barack had gotten here first, and instead of interrogating the snakes, he was soaking up the heat with them.

The three of us sat in silence. This wasn't a bad thing, necessarily — it was how many men preferred to spend their time when in the company of other men. The only things missing were a couple of cigars and a college football game on a big-screen TV.

155

The door opened. It was the masseur. I started to stand, but he shook his head. It wasn't my time yet. I had to marinate some more.

"See you ladies later," Rahm said, following the big guy out.

Once Barack and I were alone, I turned to him. "What are you doing here?" I hissed through clenched teeth.

"What are *you* doing here?"

"I needed a massage."

"So did I."

I wiped the sweat off my brow. It was beginning to drip into my eyes. "Where's your Service detail?"

"Right here, Mr. Biden," a voice called from the far end of the room. A man dressed in a full suit was sitting on the bottom bench. There was a towel hanging over his head, but I would have recognized that whiny voice anywhere.

Barack cleared his throat. "Steve had some car trouble. Didn't you, Steve?" No answer from the agent at the other end of the sauna. "You wouldn't know anything about that, would you, Joe?"

I shook my head. "It was running fine when I parked it. Legally. When I parked it legally, is what I'm trying to say."

Barack nodded but didn't press me on it.

Steve didn't say anything, either. He was in another one of his "moods." Steve sulked more than a grounded teenager during summer break. A side effect of his chronic carb deficiency.

Barack dropped his voice a few notches: "I don't know where you ran off to during my speech —"

"I didn't —"

He held a hand up to stop me. "We're both here for the same reason: to pump Rahm for everything he knows about this police investigation into the Denton shooting. He says the Chicago PD is focused on the parades and whatnot. The shooting at the freight yard is only one of several shootings so far. You were right about the weather, Joe. When the sun goes down, they're planning for all hell to break loose. They don't have anyone to spare on detective work on a day like this. Gangland shootings —"

"You believe that? That he was in a gang? Because Pastor Brown didn't seem to think so."

"It doesn't matter what I believe. It matters what the police believe. They looked at his iPhone. No texts or calls this morning to suggest he was meeting somebody at the freight yard. They have one lead right now, and that's the gun used in the shooting."

"They found it," I said.

"They found a spent casing. They entered its unique identifier into a ballistics database that tracks guns used in violent crimes and found a match: a Glock used in a shooting in Los Angeles several years ago. The serial number, plugged into a different database, gave them the owner's name and address. A dealer. That's where the trail went cold. The Glock had been on a shipment from Kansas City to Philadelphia when it went missing."

My hope began to fade. "Missing."

Barack nodded. "Three weeks ago, thieves broke into a couple different cargo containers at Norfolk Southern. They made off with half a million dollars in firearms, which have slowly been turning up on the streets. This is the first one used in a crime. It won't be the last."

"Jesus." Chicago could ban handgun sales within its borders, but everybody knew you couldn't stop the influx of guns on your own. You needed cooperation — from neighboring states, from the Feds. Cooperation that we all knew would never happen. "I take it they haven't found the thieves."

"The investigation was stalled out," Barack said. "This could be the break they've been waiting for."

"I don't follow."

"Rahm thinks Shaun was involved in the cargo burglary. It's too much of a co-incidence, otherwise. One of the missing guns shows up at the same freight yard it was stolen from? I have to admit, from where Rahm is sitting, I'd draw the same conclusion."

"What about from where you're sitting?"

"I'm trying to be objective," he said. "I told him about the stolen BlackBerry, and how you were only trying to help me out by going after it. Rahm said to check back on Monday, see where things settle."

The bottom of my stomach dropped out. Rahm already looked at me like I was a schmuck.

"You didn't have to tell him about your connection," I said.

"No, you're right. I didn't have to. But I wanted to. What's more important: my reputation or seeing justice served?"

"Your reputation? What about mine?"

"Same question."

I grumbled under my breath. Words I won't repeat. The gist was that he was right — it didn't matter if it was his reputation, mine, or the man in the moon's. If it helped bring the perpetrator to justice, then it was worth it. In the end, it was worth it.

The Secret Service had finished their

review of the video from the Tribune Tower security cameras. They knew the names and faces of everyone who was supposed to be in the building — the conference, the newsroom employees upstairs. The office tenants who leased space in the building.

"Bottom line is, nobody unknown to the Secret Service slipped into that building," Barack said. "If Shaun didn't steal my phone . . ."

"It could have been anyone, practically."

Barack explained that the Service's investigators were cross-referencing the list of everyone who had building access with multiple criminal databases. They'd already completed this step before the conference but were double-checking now in case there had been a security lapse on their part. I didn't think so. Half the volunteers from Pastor Brown's church would have thrown up red flags but had been approved by Barack personally. If it was a lapse on anyone's part, it wasn't the Secret Service's.

"We all make mistakes," I said.

Barack raised an eyebrow.

"I wasn't talking about you," I said. "I was talking about those kids in Pastor Brown's congregation. You weren't wrong to place your trust in them. It's possible to screw up and turn things around."

160

"You're right," he said, his eyes focused on some spot on the floor. He'd spoken about his teenage years many times. Written about them. I couldn't wrap my mind around the stuff he'd done — the drugs. The drinking. But he'd grown up. He was a different man now. He didn't need to be reminded that the penalty for such behavior wasn't getting shot in the back and left for dead.

The door opened again. Another large man. He nodded to me. There was a bundle of birch branches in his right hand. What sort of massage was this?

I rose to my feet and went light-headed. I'd forgotten all the warning signs they post about spending too much time in saunas and steam rooms. Especially if you're on the backside of fifty.

"We're not through talking," I told Barack once I'd steadied myself. "You're not going to run off on me, are you?"

"You're the one who ran off on me."

"I can see how it might look that way."

"Don't try to pull that 'fake news' bull on me, Joe. It looks that way because that's what you did. When I went onstage, you snuck out to do a little digging around on your own."

"I would have asked you to come with,

but . . ." I nodded in the direction of Steve. Our erstwhile babysitter, whose shoulders were slumping.

"How you doin' down there, Steve?" Barack shouted.

The masseur who'd come for me followed our eyes to Steve, who, as if on cue, collapsed on the bench in a puddle of his own sweat. It took us all a moment to react. We should have seen it coming, though. Nobody wears a full suit into a sauna. I knew why he hadn't wanted to undress: he was concerned that President Obama's abs would be more numerous and defined than his own. It was also possible that he had wanted to keep his government-issued firearm hidden, preferring not to walk through the baths with a shoulder holster. He was right to be wary about leaving his weapon and phone in the locker room. Even under lock and key. You couldn't be too careful around Russians these days.

24

Steve's breathing was shallow and ragged as we helped the masseur carry him out. And when I say "helped," I mean "watched him carry Steve like a sack of beans." The brute hauled his limp body to one of the massage beds in the middle of the room. Rahm was facedown on the next bed, getting worked over like a raw steak. His pink cheeks were sticking up in the air. There was no privacy in the Russian baths — every man and woman was equal, wearing nothing but his or her own skin. And, sometimes, a towel.

"Help me out, Joe?" Barack asked.

He was busy removing Steve's jacket. Steve was mumbling incoherently. We had to cool him down. The fastest way to do that was to strip him to his skivvies. You ever try to take off another man's pants? It's not as easy as it sounds.

"This reminds me of this one time at Archmere," I said, struggling to get Steve out of his slacks. One of his knees — they were very bony — kept catching.

"Joe," Barack said, "if I hear one more story about your weird 1930s all-boys prep school, I'm going to lose it. We're going to have quiet time. Whoever can stay silent the longest gets two scoops of chocolate-chip ice cream."

"And a waffle cone?"

"And a waffle cone," he said. "We start now."

"If you think I can't shut up for five minutes, then —"

"You're still talking."

Five minutes. I could shut up for five minutes. It's not like I was some motor mouth, narrating my own story and diving off on tangents. Not like that Joe Biden caricature in that hack's mystery novel. Gadzooks, what a fool he'd made me out to be! A one-dimensional clown. I'd graduated at the top of my class.

The top fifty percent.

We helped Steve onto the massage bed. His skin was pale and clammy. Not because of the sauna. Pale and clammy was his natural state. He was always going on about "sweating out the toxins," which left him in a perpetually disgusting condition as far as his pores were concerned.

Barack rubbed his own chin. I guessed his mind was covering the same ground as mine: *Do we call an ambulance or take Steve to the hospital ourselves?* What he needed was fluids to replace all the sweat. And toxins. A man needs toxins in his bloodstream. It's not good to sweat them all out.

The masseur was back with a fifth of vodka — either for himself or for Steve, I had no idea.

"He'll be A-OK," the man said. He had an Eastern European accent, and his English was as broken as the European Union these days. "One hour rest. He's a little guy, so maybe longer."

I slipped my red bracelet onto Steve's wrist. "He can have my massage."

Barack's eyebrows peaked. I held my breath, waiting for him to remind me it hadn't been five minutes of quiet time yet. Instead, he said, "That's very generous of you."

"It might help him get back on his feet sooner."

Barack crouched down next to Rahm. "Hey, can you watch over our friend here for a while? We'll be right back."

"Where are you going?" Rahm asked, his voice muffled by the pillow. The masseur was pounding his back like a drum.

"Joe and I are going out for ice cream."

25

Barack Obama is a goshdarned liar.

How do I know? Because he admitted as much to me. After we dressed and snuck out the back door, I asked him where we were going to get ice cream. According to my phone there was a Jeni's Splendid Ice Cream within walking distance.

"Put that away," Barack said, looking left and then right as we hurried down the alley. There were no Secret Service agents guarding him. It had just been Steve and him, and now it was Barack and me.

"You know where it's at?" I said. "Great. I can never follow the maps on this damned thing. It tells you to go north, but how do you know which way north is? Sometimes it points you there, other times it spins you in circles and you end up walking round and round until you say forget it, forget the whole damn thing, modern technology isn't for me. Don't you think your life was easier before?"

"Before cellphones? On the one hand, yes. On the other hand, I don't think I would have given up my BlackBerry for Lent if I didn't always have the Secret Service or Michelle or my kids with me with their phones. What if there's a medical emergency? What if you need the police?"

"That's a lot of what ifs," I said.

Barack thrust his hands into his pockets. I had to race to keep up with him — the man has long legs, and everybody knows that gives you an unfair advantage in a footrace. We weren't racing, but he was still moving as fast as he could without bending his knees. A mall-walker's pace.

"What happened to your windbreaker? We can't go into Jeni's looking like ourselves," I said. "We'll be mobbed by fans. Or I will be, because that's my go-to ice cream joint."

"We're not going to Jeni's."

"You know someplace with better ice cream? It's not that I don't believe you, it's just that it's an allegation I can't buy without seeing the underlying science."

"We're not getting ice cream, Joe."

That's how he said it: just like that. A statement of fact, as if I should have known the whole time. Barack never intended to get ice cream. It was a ruse all along.

"If we're not getting ice cream, then may I ask where we're going?"

"You can ask," Barack said.

"Consider this me asking."

"We're going to find some answers," he said without slowing. "Can you keep up?"

"Can I — ?" I jogged after him.

"It's not far. We'll stick to the back alleys."

He seemed fine to leave it at that. To leave me — his supposed best friend, his pal, his brother — in the dark, if not in the dust.

We ducked behind an overflowing trash bin that hadn't been emptied since the Daley administration. The first one. A gaggle of young folks stumbled past on the sidewalk. They turned into a bar on the corner, even though they already seemed plenty inebriated. This whole "going from one bar to another" made no sense to me. Didn't they serve the same beer at every bar? What were they chasing?

Barack looked both ways for traffic and then waved me on across the street. I followed him down another alley between two rows of brownstones. There were more signs posted warning us not to feed the rats. It might have been my imagination, but I swore the clip-art rats were getting bigger.

"Maybe we should turn around," I said.

"You don't think we owe it to Shaun to

find him justice? This was your idea, Joe."

"I'm worried about Steve."

"You're worried. About Steve."

"Physically he's tough as nails," I said, "but he has some trust issues." This wasn't the first time we'd ditched him.

"So you're not worried about his health, you're worried about his feelings."

"There's only so far you can push a man before he breaks."

I was talking about me, if that wasn't clear. Barack knew it. He wasn't a master at picking up on subtext, but we shared a bond. Unfortunately, we were building walls between us. I hadn't told him about visiting the Red Door; he hadn't told me he was going to the Russian baths. My cabbie had told me the snakes would be coming out as the temperature climbed. For the first time, I wondered if we weren't a couple of snakes ourselves.

We crossed over into a mostly residential neighborhood with a smattering of high-end boutiques, restaurants, and art studios. Wicker Park, according to Barack. There were thick steel bars on the lower-level windows of every residence. It seemed like a nightmare way to live your life, always peering out from behind bars like you were a prisoner in your own home. The houses couldn't have been cheap, but each one was a prison. A multimillion-dollar prison.

Halfway down a block of retail establishments, Barack stopped so abruptly that I bumped into him. He looked a four-story brick building up and down. THE RECORD STORE, a faded sign in the first-floor window announced. What drew my ire, however, were the signs for "smoking accessories," whatever those were. Lighters, I assumed. If Barack had marched me a quarter of a mile from the Russian baths to grab a pack of smokes, I was going to lose it. He had quit. I didn't want to be part of his falling off the wagon.

"We don't have time for ice cream but we have time for this?" I said. "That's why you didn't want to tell me where we were headed, because you knew I'd say no."

"I'm going to need you to stay outside, act as a lookout."

"So you can buy a pack of smokes?"

"It's a record store. You ever been to a record store?"

"Sure," I said. "They used to carry 45s at Danny Eaton's dime store in Scranton. Me and my brothers —"

Barack went inside, leaving me behind on the sidewalk.

He was in the shop for less than a minute before I followed him.

26

Inside, the Record Store was dingy and damp. Sunlight hadn't come through the poster-covered front windows in years. Every footstep released some new, awful smell from the carpet. A biologist studying funguses and spores could have spent a lifetime cataloging new growths, provided they were brave enough to don a hazmat suit and rip up the carpeting.

The man behind the register had a long beard and an even longer ponytail. He was smoking a cigarette, pricing records and paying no attention as I scooted past him. You weren't supposed to smoke inside *any* retail business these days, as far as I knew. Chicagoans didn't seem to care much what you were and weren't supposed to do. At one time, the city had been the springboard for western expansion. It still had a bit of that Wild West attitude. Barack and his Chicago crew — including Rahm and Axe

— had ridden into Washington like they were gunslingers in a Clint Eastwood western. Behind the scenes, I had to play the killjoy sheriff, letting them know from time to time that they weren't half as clever as they thought.

Barack was flipping through vinyl records with a grin on his face, nodding along to a rap song overhead. I crept up beside him. There were a couple stacks of CDs here and there, but the majority of the stock was devoted to vinyl. We were the only two customers.

"I thought we were here for a reason," I said.

"Mmmmm-hmmmm."

"A reason related to the case."

"Mmmmm-hmmmm."

"You're just going to keep saying that until I give up, aren't you?"

"Mmmmm-hmmmm."

He started humming along to the chorus of the song. Hip-hop wasn't my bowl of chili, so I couldn't tell you the artist's name. I still remember the first hip-hop song I'd ever heard. Tipper Gore had played it for me on a Walkman. She was shaking her head the whole time, and then afterward asked if I wasn't moved to do something about it. *I'm moved to turn it off,* I joked.

Wasn't I offended, she wanted to know? Didn't I want to *do something*? I told her that I hadn't understood a damn word but that the First Amendment covered a multitude of sins.

I later found out the cassette tape in question had been Al's.

"Doesn't it stink in here?" I whispered to Barack. "Do you smell that?"

He drew in a deep breath through his nose, eyes closed. "It smells like a record store, Joe. I used to spend hours in here — not at this location, but when it was in Hyde Park."

"Did that one smell as bad as this one?"

"Worse."

He picked out a record and flipped it over, reading the track list. I poked my head over his shoulder to get a glimpse. I was hovering like my agents used to when I would make an unscheduled stop at a Dairy Queen in small-town America.

"Why don't you go ask how much this one is?" he said, handing the record to me.

I looked it over. *Tha Drilluminati.* Caruso. The rapper was shirtless on the cover, his body covered in skull-and-cross-bones tats. So different from his older self. What shocked me the most was that vinyl had outlived eight-tracks and cassette tapes. Live long enough, and everything old will become new again. Not that I ever paid much attention to music formats. If a tune came on the radio that I liked, I would turn it up a notch. I enjoyed music, but I didn't feel the need to blow my money on it. In contrast, Barack often boasted of his record collection in mixed company, like he'd written and performed the songs himself. He didn't have a favorite Marvin Gaye song — he had a list of his top fifty Marvin Gaye songs.

I slapped the record down on the glass countertop to get Mr. Ponytail's attention. He looked up from his stack. When his eyes met mine, he did a double take. More like a triple take: confusion, recognition, confusion.

"My friend wants to know how much this is," I said.

Mr. Ponytail slowly turned his head toward Barack. When he realized who "my friend" was, the cigarette fell from his lips into a pile of ash on the counter.

27

Mr. Ponytail had a name. Morrison. He'd been managing the Record Store for over forty years — first in Hyde Park and then at the current location. Rents were rising across the city, he explained. How long they'd last here was anyone's guess. It was the same story I'd been hearing in medium to large cities across the country. Residents and businesses were being pushed out in the name of progress.

"Doesn't sound very progressive to me," I said. The three of us had retired to the back room.

"Woke Joe Biden," Morrison said. "I love it."

I watched him carefully, trying to determine if he was making fun of me. He looked like he was trying to suppress a smile. Or maybe he was just high on the pot.

"As much as I'd love to continue this discussion," Barack said, "we're not here to talk neoliberal policies and their effects on the urban retail landscape."

"No, no, of course not," Morrison said.

I peeked into the store through the curtains. It was empty, same as we'd left it.

"Did you hear something?" Barack asked.

I shook my head. "The front door is locked. You're sure?"

Morrison nodded. He was looking at me like I was being paranoid.

I probably was. Nobody had followed us from the Russian baths. I'd been looking over my shoulder half the time, so much that I kept bumping into telephone poles. But somebody had to keep an eye out. The leprechaun hadn't been some figment of my imagination — I wasn't that imaginative. Steve had seen him. I had every right to be paranoid. Perhaps Barack was right, though. He'd told me Rahm was just concerned about my safety. But if he'd been concerned enough to put that leprechaun on my trail, what would he do when he realized Barack was wandering around Chicago sans Secret Service.

"Are you expecting visitors?" Morrison said.

"There was a shooting today in Englewood," Barack said. "A boy is in the hospital. The police ran a database search on the ballistics and traced the gun. It was reported stolen from a shipping container in the freight yard — the same place the shooting took place. A couple weeks back."

"This town, man."

"We're looking for information on the robbery," Barack said. I nodded along, as if I had any idea where he was going with this.

Morrison lit up another smoke. "How is it you think I can help? I mean, I'll do anything, but I'm not following what it is you want."

Barack cleared his throat. "Morrie. C'mon, man."

The hippie wiped his eyeglasses with his shirt. He peered through them at the fluorescent ceiling light — the storage room was better lit than the front — and, unsatisfied with his cleaning job, wiped them again.

"You know I don't mess with no guns," Morrison said.

"Neither do I," Barack said. "But you're selling more than records. You always have. This neighborhood isn't where most people displaced by gentrification end up. You've got to be paying more than you were in Hyde Park."

"Are you wearing wires? If this is a sting, you have to tell me."

Barack waved his hand to clear the smoke.

"The federal government did not send the president and vice president into a record store to entrap somebody. The federal government has better things to do than waste time on low-level dealers."

"Like aliens," Morrison said.

"Wait —" I said, trying to interject some sense of normalcy into the conversation.

Morrison jumped right back in. "Roswell. You know what really happened. Tell me and I'll help you however I can."

"The official story is that, in 1947, a military surveillance balloon crashed on a ranch outside Roswell, New Mexico," Barack said. "If, hypothetically, the United States government recovered evidence of extraterrestrial life from a flying saucer at the crash site, that would be top secret. Only the president and a few others would have that type of clearance. Joe doesn't even have access to information like that."

I nodded. "He won't even tell *me* if aliens are real or not. You really expect President Obama to tell *you* —"

Barack held up an arm to cut me off. "It's OK, Joe. Let me handle this." He turned back to Morrison. "If I tell you the truth, you'll give us what we want?"

Morrison's eyes were wandering. He must have been high — not that I'd know what that was like, but his pupils were enlarged, his eyes were pink as pink elephants, and he was tuned to a station I couldn't pick up.

"What do you have to trade?" Barack asked.

"I know people," Morrison said, suddenly lucid. "I'm not in the black market anymore — I'm being straight with you, man — but I know people."

"I know people, too," Barack said.

I rubbed my temples. The cigarette smoke was getting to me. Either that or I was about to have another aneurysm on account of this guy trying to weasel his way out of providing us anything of value.

Morrison cleared his throat. "You're looking to trace this gun, right? But it's not that easy. Black market dealers don't keep track of the serial numbers on the guns they sell. Trying to pinpoint a single gun is like trying to find a needle in a halfway house. If that's your only lead, even if you can trace it back to who stole this shipment, the trail's going to go cold fast. Unless . . ."

"Unless?" Barack said.

"How long ago was this cargo hold knocked off?"

"About three weeks ago."

Morrison nodded. "I think I heard about that. Half a million in firearms. If the thieves

181

were local, there's no way they could fence that many weapons on the street all at once. Not by themselves."

"Why do you say that?"

"It was all there in the *Sun-Times*. If it's the same one I'm thinking of, they hit three different containers, stealing stuff left and right. On the third one, they hit the mother lode. They weren't expecting them guns to be there, see? They were after whatever they could get. They're probably still sitting on the guns, selling one or two here and there, but they can't pawn them. They definitely don't have an organization across state lines to distribute them because that would mean going back up the food chain. My guess is it was a local crew who hit the freight yard. Happens all the time. They wouldn't know what to do with them, so they're just sitting on them."

"You don't know for sure," Barack said.

"If the guns had hit the streets all at once, word would have gotten out, prices would have been driven down temporarily. Gangs are businesses. Some of the leaders these days have MBAs. They're the scariest of all — they've got the smarts, they're ruthless." He paused. "But the guys on the bottom rung are sloppy. Overaggressive. They're kids, so what do you expect? Whoever shot your friend probably did it in the heat of the moment. The gang leaders don't like shootings — they're bad for business. Leaving evidence behind that ballistics can trace? Your shooter could have just put their entire weapons cache at risk. If you can nail down the gang who committed the burglary, the leadership will do the legwork for you and find the shooter. Especially if he's one of their own."

"Which gang hit the freight yard?" I asked.

"How should I know? I'm just telling you what I read in the paper, man."

Morrison started to light another cigarette, and I snatched the lighter from his hands.

"I've half a mind to cut that damn ponytail of yours."

Barack held me back. "Joe —"

"Wait," Morrison said. "Nobody gets away with a robbery like that without the cops getting their cut. People in the neighborhood talk. Informants talk. Somebody in a squad car has taken a pay-off to keep the heat turned down, to bury this thing."

"Crooked cops," I said. Been there, done that.

"Just 'cops,' " Morrison said. "Calling them crooked in this town is an oxymoron."

"You mean 'redundant,' " Barack said.

I pocketed the lighter. "Nobody's going to

cross the thin blue line to talk to us. I'm already in hot water with the mayor's fixer. If we go sniffing around, asking questions like what you're asking, we could wind up in Chicago overcoats. Six feet under."

Barack shot me a perturbed look. "Chicago overcoats? The last person to actually say that out loud was John Dillinger. Just say coffins, Joe. Coffins."

I grunted an acknowledgment of his request but by no means a *yessir.* Barack had asked me to be part of his campaign in 2008 because he wasn't looking for a "yes man." I wasn't about to start now.

I was, however, going to brush up on my Chicago slang when I had a chance.

"I suppose you've got a plan for getting us this insider information," Barack said.

Morrison nodded enthusiastically. "Cops talk. All you have to do is follow the trail of loose lips. And like I told you, I know people."

I couldn't believe Barack was seriously entertaining this fool. Where did he get off using top secret information as a bargaining chip? I'd been in government longer than he had. I'd been chairman of the foreign relations committee before he could even walk. This wasn't the first time Barack had teased me with his superior clearance level.

184

One of his favorite sayings was, *Only one of us knows what happened in Roswell, Joe.*

Morrison scribbled a name and address on a Subway napkin. There was a half-eaten meatball sub on white sitting on the computer desk, next to a laptop.

I took the napkin, expecting it to read THE RED DOOR.

It didn't.

"Gal Capone, the alley," I read aloud. "Which alley?"

"It's a club," he said. "The Alley. A speakeasy on Broadway. You can find the cross street online. Some of the guys who come in here talk about it."

"Gal Capone?" Barack said.

"Gal owns the place. If anyone can help you on the down-low, it's Gal. She's got girls on her payroll in every ward. But you have to understand: I can't guarantee you'll like what you find."

"There are no guarantees in life," Barack said, rising to his feet.

Morrison stared at him expectantly. "Well?"

"Well?" Barack repeated. "Joe and I need to get on the road and check this out. Thank you for your help. Now if —"

"No, the thing. The thing you said you'd tell me."

185

"Oh, right," Barack said, as if he'd simply forgotten his end of the bargain. I'd known all along that he never intended to tell the store manager a damned thing about Roswell, aliens or otherwise. Classified information was classified for a reason. You couldn't go around trading it for favors whenever it benefited you personally. Even if you were doing it for the right reasons.

Barack told me to head on out, that he'd catch up with me in a second.

I waited at the front of the store. Thirty seconds passed. I looked outside through a small break in the posters. Nobody out there. I'd expected the Secret Service, or Rahm's man in green. But there was nobody following us. Nobody but our own shadows.

28

Barack joined me in the front of the store and handed me a stocking cap. He put one on — gifts from our new friend.

There were, Barack had once told me, two truly spectacular months in Chicago: June and October. Today wasn't bad, though. You couldn't ask for better weather to do a little amateur detective work in.

I knew it wasn't going to last. When the front passed, another long, deep freeze would set in that wouldn't lift until April or May, and only then to make way for freezing rain. God bless Chicago, they still played baseball outdoors. The way America's pastime was meant to be played. Playing indoors was blasphemy, like low-fat ice cream.

While we waited on a cab, I asked Barack what he'd told Morrison.

"About Roswell?" Barack said. "You know I can't tell you that, Joe. That's classified information, on a need-to-know basis. You're better off not knowing."

"You're saying that you told him? The truth?"

The taxi interrupted us, and Barack didn't say another word about it. I didn't want to bring it up, even with the closed partition between us and the driver. By the time we reached our destination, I had other mysteries on my mind.

The address we'd found online turned out to be a laundromat in the middle of a block of low-rise brick buildings. I looked from my phone to the address and back again. "GPS says this is it. Maybe it closed down?"

Barack rubbed his chin. "Could be in an alley behind the building. Or . . ."

He went inside without completing his thought.

Three commercial dryers were running. A college-age girl was sitting at a table, head down in a Gillian Flynn paperback. Barack marched right on through the laundromat. He stopped at a navy-blue police phone-call kiosk, the freestanding kind they used to have in Great Britain. It was tucked into a corner. Was there a phone inside that connected to the Chicago PD? Had the longhair sent us here on some sort of wild moose chase?

Barack opened the kiosk and turned to me. "Ever been to a speakeasy?"

"Just how old do you think I am?"

"I'll let you go first," he said, ushering me into the box. It was bigger on the inside than it looked, and opened to a wide staircase leading up to the second floor. A single light — an "Edison" bulb — hung from the ceiling on the landing, giving off a warm orange glow.

I pounded on the metal door at the top of the steps, eager to get this over with. We shouldn't have shrugged off Barack's Service detail. Who knew what was lurking behind this door? We could have been walking into a trap. Now that we weren't tethered to security, we were exposed. Naked. Not as naked as I'd been in the sauna, but close to it.

"What happens when there's a fire, and the fire department doesn't think to go through a phone booth looking for an address?" I asked Barack. "How do all these businesses in Chicago make money without signs? Who are they trying to fool?"

"I'd imagine that if there's a fire, they'd follow the smoke." He paused. "But, you know, this city doesn't have a great track record with fires, so maybe you're on to something."

189

I pounded again. And waited.

"I'd feel better about this if I had some hardware," I whispered.

He cast me a sidelong glance. "Your guns are locked up at home right now, aren't they? Tell me you're a responsible gun owner, Joe."

"You can't go out on a book tour armed to your teeth."

"I believe Hunter S. Thompson tried that once."

He wasn't somebody I'd read in college. "How'd that work out for him?"

Barack chuckled. "His pistol went off during one of his readings. Same bookstore you were in earlier today, if you can believe it. Shot the hat off some poor fellow seated in the back row."

"Was he OK?"

"The guy who'd been shot? I don't know. Hunter was pissed when his literary agent confiscated the gun."

"Terrible accident."

"Oh, it wasn't an accident," Barack said. "He was shooting at a copy of Nixon's autobiography."

"Makes sense," I said, though none of it did. We'd clearly been to some very different book readings over the years.

Finally the door creaked open. A bald

head poked out. It belonged to a weak-jawed man with a black goatee and too much eyeliner. He even had a couple of tiny metal studs on his forehead. Horns. It'd taken me seventy-six years to look the devil in the eye, and I could barely keep a straight face.

"Yessssssssss?" he said, drawing out the S so that he sounded like a snake hissing.

"We're here for the early show," Barack said.

"There is no early show," Beelzebubba said. "The Alley is closed. We open at nine, at which time —"

"Step aside," I said. "We're here to see Ms. Capone."

"Everyone comes for Madam Capone," he said with a wink, as if he'd just invented puns. I'd heard worse on the Senate floor.

I stuck my foot between the door and the frame.

He sneered at me. "I am sorry, sirs, we are closed —"

"Not today, Satan," I said, wrenching the door from him and opening it wide enough for Barack and me to barge in. Beelzebubba tripped backward over his own feet, then scurried off down a narrow hallway like a spooked cockroach. He disapeared around a corner.

Barack shook his head. "Chicago goths."

29

I took the lead, marching us down the first of many labyrinthine hallways in pursuit of Beelzebubba. More old-timey bulbs lit the way. I couldn't tell if it was an interior decorating choice, or just an indication of how long the Alley had been in operation. Was there a fire exit, or was the staircase we'd come up the only way in and out of the club? How much had they paid off an inspector to approve an arrangement such as this? I was genuinely curious. In Wilmington, you couldn't put up a treehouse without a permit.

"I bet they don't even have a liquor license," I said.

"That would certainly lend some authenticity to the speakeasy vibe," Barack said. I thought I heard admiration in his voice. "The Prohibition era was interesting. Many parallels to today, if you think about it. We're fighting some of the same fights —

the growing divide between urban and rural Americans, the rising anti-immigrant fervor. The Moral Majority. We're repeating the past."

"Nothing ever changes," I said.

"Some things change. Civil rights, equality. I'm talking about the patterns we're doomed to repeat. If you take the long view of human history . . ."

He droned on. There wasn't any way to get a word in when Barack Obama was in professor mode. I knew exactly what he was talking about, anyway. A hundred years ago, the Irish had been the immigrant boogeymen. The popular image of the leprechaun began life as a xenophobic political cartoon. Once, nobody thought a Catholic could be president. Then Kennedy came along. From time to time, we liked to pat ourselves on the back and think we were done with hate. Recent history had shown us it didn't take much to awaken it, though.

We rounded the bend and found ourselves in a candlelit room with a handful of empty tables. It was roughly the size of my first college dorm, where we'd squeezed in two guys (and a couple girls on the weekends).

A spotlight switched on, illuminating a stage at the front of the room. A black curtain, serving as a backdrop, was swaying slightly.

I tapped Barack on the arm. "Over there," I said, pointing to the stage.

He swatted my hand away. "I'm not blind, Joe."

A trumpet sounded, a snare kicked in. A bass joined them. A jazz trio was playing — not live, but the sound reproduction was so crisp you could have fooled me. It had to be a Bose system. Nobody did audio like Bose.

"Welcome to the stage the one, the only, Gal Capone!"

Barack took a seat at the table nearest the stage, and I followed suit. I searched around for Beelzebubba, but the spotlight made it difficult to see anything else in the club.

"I have a bad feeling about this," I whispered to Barack.

He shushed me like I'd blurted the winning lottery numbers in the middle of a Wawa. Before I could tell him to knock it off, the curtain parted. A woman emerged, stepping onto the stage one long leg after another, each in fishnet stockings. Her skin was ivory, blinding in the spotlight, her hair and lips cherry red like a '67 Corvette straight off the assembly line. She was wearing a sparkling, diamond-encrusted bikini top and bottom . . . and nothing else. Her eyes were closed as she stalked the stage, writhing in slow motion to the music.

"This reminds me of a bachelor party I once went to. You know Bob Dole? Well, it was 1975, and —"

Barack shushed me again. The look on his face said it all. Too bad. It was quite the story, and I couldn't guarantee I'd be in the mood to tell him later —

Something smacked me in the face and fell into my lap.

The dancer's glittering top.

Slowly, I looked up and was relieved to see that Gal wasn't topless. She was wearing pasties, which were made entirely of red sequins. I say "relieved" because I wasn't sure if I'd be able to look Jill in the eye had I been patronizing a club of ill repute, where women pranced around in their birthday suits. Had Barack known what type of club this was ahead of time? He'd seemed awfully certain about entering through the phone booth . . .

I was about to risk him shushing me again when Gal slid off the stage and cartwheeled toward us, landing in one magnificent, fluid motion. The spotlight followed her. She stood tall over me and held out a palm.

I tried to hand back her top, but she shook

her head.

"I think she wants you to dance with her," Barack said, smirking.

"No thanks," I said. "I'm not much of a dancer."

She stuck out her bottom lip, making a pouty face. I'd never been susceptible to such female manipulations. It wasn't going to work on me.

"My friend's got some moves," I said. "You ever watch the first Inaugural Ball? Barack —"

His eyes went wide. *Ix-nay* on our *amesnay.*

Before I could change up my story, she switched her focus to Barack, staring at him expectantly. The smirk dropped from his face. I knew there was no way in Sam Hill he was getting up on that stage with this woman, even if we were the only ones in the room. For one thing, if Michelle found out —

Barack rose and nearly tipped over.

"Everything OK?" I asked. At first I suspected he'd been drugged, but we hadn't had anything to drink. Then I followed Barack's eyes down to his chair — his shins were tied to the legs with rope. I made a move to help him out but found that my own legs wouldn't move either. While we'd been entranced by the show, Gal's master of ceremonies had tied us up. Beelzebubba, emerging from under our table, tossed the end of the rope up to his partner, and before Barack and I could react, he'd turned our chairs around so that we were back to back. Gal Capone flung the rope around us, round and round, up and down, trapping our arms against our bodies until we were bound like hogs on the way to market.

30

"So, you come here often?"

I could feel Barack twist his head behind me. "Joe, now's not the time."

We were alone, tied up in the middle of the blackened club. The spotlight had been turned off. Gal and Beelzebubba had disappeared without a word, despite my adamant protestations.

We'd been sitting back to back for at least fifteen minutes. I tried to twist my arm so that I could get a look at my watch, but the ropes were too tight to allow even that little bit of movement. Every time I pushed back, they seemed to constrict like an anaconda. I'd have bet money she'd used a modified Miller's knot.

"We walked right into that one," I said, shaking my head. "Did you ever think for one minute that we were walking straight into a trap?"

"It crossed my mind," Barack said.

"And you didn't say anything?"

"I assumed it had crossed your mind as well."

"It did, but you know what happens when you assume."

"What happens, Joe?"

"This," I said through gritted teeth. *"This."*

"It's going to be OK. Relax."

"You have a plan?" I whispered.

"I think it's pretty clear that I don't. If I did, we would have already turned the tables on these goofballs."

"Damn. I thought maybe you had planned to get caught."

"That's not a very good plan, Joe."

"I didn't think so, but I was holding out hope. You're supposed to be the one who's never caught off guard. You're the cool guy. I'm the hothead. Remember?"

He didn't say anything. The music had long since stopped, but my ears were still ringing. The club was a small, intimate space, and the jazz had been cranked to eleven.

"Nothing?" I said.

"You know, I'm getting tired of hearing that I'm the 'cool guy.' "

"It's a compliment."

"You want to know why I wore the tan suit today?" he asked.

"You had a stroke?"

"It's because I'm tired of being the Cool President. I want to be myself again. Being the Cool President means I'm smart (but not too smart), funny (but not too funny). It means I know what 420 is and can name every member of both the Beatles and One Direction. The Cool President enjoys the taste of craft beer but knows there's a time and a place for everything — if I'm in the bleachers at Wrigley, God forbid, it's Old Milwaukee Time or GTFO. And, yeah, the Cool President drops a naughty acronym every once in a while.

"And before some word nerd points it out, I know that's technically an initialism and not an acronym. IDGAF.

"The Cool President never gets angry. Ever. Getting mad isn't cool. It's the opposite — that's why it's called 'losing your cool.' Go ahead and interrupt my State of the Union. Call me names on Twitter. Call me a Kenyan. You can't provoke me because Barack don't crack.

"There's a fallacy in all of this, of course: politics isn't cool. Running for office — even the highest office in the land — isn't cool. The Cool President is as carefully calculated a creation as fast-food fries. If you ever wanted to see me lose my temper

200

in the White House, all you would have had to do was attend one of our pick-up basketball games. I dropped the Cool President facade on the court. Elbow me in the face? Oh, it was on. Those were the moments I lived for.

"I was a college professor before getting into politics. I wrote a book — that nobody bought. I was a nerd. The Cool President was just someone I was pretending to be. I thought that if I put the tan suit on, I could shed that image."

"And the green socks."

"What's wrong with the green socks?"

While I understood where he was coming from, being the Cool President had its advantages. If he had his BlackBerry, for instance, he could have reached out to Bradley Cooper for help. It was easy to imagine the A-list actor busting through the wall, guitar in hand, and setting us free, all without messing up a single perfect hair on his perfect head.

"He didn't change his number, did he?" I said.

"Who didn't change his number?"

"You know who."

Barack let out a long sigh. "He changed his number, but . . ."

"But you have his new number."

201

"I'm sorry, Joe. I don't know what to say. The whole jealousy thing is getting old. This isn't high school."

"You think I'm jealous of him? Mr. Hollywood? Puhlease."

"I'm not the one who keeps bringing him up."

"I'm wondering why you would lie to me."

"Because I knew you were going to act like this, Joe. And I was right, wasn't I?"

There was a long pause. "This is what they're hoping we do, isn't it?" I said. "Turn against each other."

"I don't know what they want."

"We're in a big dill pickle. It's not like we haven't been here before, though. Not literally, of course."

"We've never been tied up. We've never been kidnapped."

"We've had some close calls, though," I said. "Say, don't you have some sort of presidential locator microchip implanted under your skin? I meant to ask you if they —"

"No, I don't."

"The technology's kind of creepy, but it would be nice to have, wouldn't it?"

"I've never thought about it, honestly. We don't need a locator chip, though: you have your cellphone on you. At some point, Steve will become curious. He can trace us using that."

"It's a pay-as-you-go phone. I never registered it online."

"Joe?"

"Yeah?"

"If this is it — if this is the end . . ."

"Don't talk like that. Don't you talk like that."

"I'm serious, Joe. If this is the end, I want you to know something. I swore I'd never say it, but . . ." He paused. He sounded choked up. "Joe, hear me out, OK? I want you to know . . ."

"I'm listening. Whatever it is, you can tell me. We're friends."

"A-hem." It wasn't Barack talking now. The spotlight was back on, this time trained on us. I couldn't see if Gal was alone or if that creep was with her. She moved in the shadows on the other side of the light, slinking around like a cat on the prowl. "Am I interrupting something?"

"You're not going to get away with this," I said. "Let us go right now, and maybe we'll forget about the whole thing. It's the only way you walk out of here."

"If I were you, I'd be more concerned about yourselves walking out of here."

"You know why we're here," Barack said.

"Actually, I don't," Gal said.

"Playing dumb?" I said. "Ha. I invented playing dumb. You can't fool me."

"I'm not trying to fool you," she said. "In fact, I didn't even know who you were when you barged in here. Now that I do know who you are, I have a dilemma. If I let you go, my club will be raided and I'll spend the night in jail."

"Just the night?" I asked.

"I have good lawyers," she said. "But I don't know what else to do with you."

"You're not going to silence us?"

She knelt close to me and went to work on the knot. She was letting us go. I was flabbergasted, but not entirely surprised. She was a smart snickerdoodle cookie.

"What do you want from us?" I said as she untied Barack. I shook myself free and stood, rubbing my wrists where the rope had dug into my skin. There were red marks on both my arms, which I hoped would fade. Jill was used to me bumping my head. Rope marks were going to be more difficult to explain away.

"You didn't answer my question," I said. "What do —"

"What do I want from you? In exchange for letting you go?"

Barack got to his feet and let the rope fall

to the floor. We exchanged suspicious looks. Was he thinking we should run? It was difficult to know what was going through his mind on a regular day. Today was no regular day. I watched him closely, waiting for him to signal our next move with his eyes.

"I'm sorry that Victor didn't recognize you," Gal said, looping the rope like a lasso. "He's not really into politics."

"He doesn't vote?" Barack said.

"He writes in Mickey Mouse. For every office."

"A straight Disney ticket," I said.

"Every vote counts," Barack said. "When we don't vote, or throw away our vote on Bob Dylan or Mickey Mouse, our democracy suffers. If you don't think any of the candidates represent your values and your priorities, perhaps it's because fewer than one in ten people vote in primary elections. Victor needs to engage in the electoral process sooner rather than later. It doesn't take much time. Thirty minutes. Thirty minutes of his time. Is democracy worth that? When you vote, something powerful happens. Change happens. Don't leave it up to others. Stop waiting for the perfect candidate. Get out there and get involved. Ordinary citizens like you and your friend from Hot Topic have the power to change things."

"You don't have to convince me — I voted Obama/Biden in '08 and '12. I still sleep on my Obama pillow. And I named my twins after you. May I introduce you to Hope," she said, cupping her right breast, "and Change."

Out of the corner of my eye, I swear I saw Barack blush.

"You might be able to help us," he said, trying to recover his cool but failing miserably. "If you're willing."

"Anything you want," she said with a crooked smile. "And I do mean anything."

31

It didn't take Gal long to get us the information we were after. A few phone calls and she had the name of the street gang. I was expecting her to say "The Red Door."

The name she gave us was "The Crooks."

Barack didn't notice my relief, as far as I could tell. My fears that the Red Door was somehow mixed up in all this business were fading by the minute. Shaun might not have been involved at all in the shipping container burglary. He had no affiliation with the Crooks, or any other gang, if Pastor Brown was to be believed.

As we retraced our steps through the laundromat, I asked Barack if he'd known that his friend at the Record Store had sent us to a strip club.

"It's a burlesque club," Barack said.

"What's the difference?"

"She didn't take off all her clothes, did she?"

"Are you telling me strippers take off *everything*?"

"Joe."

"It's a serious question," I said.

"Are you telling me there aren't any strip clubs in Delaware?"

I shook my head. "I've never seen one."

"Look harder," he said.

I said I would, but we both knew I was bluffing. The only woman I wanted to see take her clothes off was my wife. Call me old-fashioned, but I didn't think it was right to see a woman in her birthday suit except in a bedroom. Your own bedroom, with a ring on her finger.

"I'm still confused about something," I said. "How do strippers — I'm sorry, 'burlesque' dancers — know so much about what goes on down at the police station?"

"Because Ms. Capone is also a madam. Her 'girls' are call girls. Sleep with enough cops, and you'll hear some stuff."

"You're saying cops talk in their sleep."

"That's . . . yes, that's exactly what I'm saying."

An awkward silence followed.

"It's probably time to check in with Steve," Barack said. "It takes more than a little hot air to keep that boy down."

"Or a bundle of sticks."

Barack looked at me quizzically.

"So we touch base with Steve, then what?" I asked.

"Then I've got to get ready for the VIP dinner. There will be hors d'oeuvres and desserts."

"I meant, then what regarding this tip about the Crooks? We can't just drive around until we see somebody wearing their colors —"

"Silver and black."

"— on a street corner and say, 'Take me to your leader.' "

"While I would like to see you try that, Joe, I've got another idea."

"Caruso," I said.

"He'll be at the dinner. He might be able to help us put together some of the pieces. Even though he's Shaun's mentor, I'm not sure how much help he'll be. He doesn't live in Englewood anymore. I was actually thinking of somebody else."

"Pastor Brown."

Barack met my eyes. "I know you don't trust him, Joe. I know you're skeptical that he could turn his life around, that anyone who does the kind of good he does could come from a background like his."

"You think he'll help us, that's all that matters."

"I'll get ahold of him tomorrow, feel him out."

"Tomorrow?"

"I'll see this thing through — not just for you, but for Shaun."

I thought it over. If Pastor Brown could do the heavy lifting and talk to the gang leaders, he might even come out of this my new hero. But if he couldn't, what then? I'd told Shaun I'd go around the world for him. There was no way I was stepping foot on that plane tonight.

I glanced at my watch. "If Steve picks us up within the next twenty minutes, we have just enough time to get down to the Red Door. Your VIP event doesn't start until nine."

"We'll be cutting things close."

"When have we ever not cut things close?"

I called Steve, who didn't seem at all curious where we'd run off to. I gave him the cross-streets. Fifteen minutes, he said. Then I found the number for the Red Door.

"Before you make the call," Barack said, "there's something you need to know about him. I wasn't being entirely straight with you about his past. I wasn't sure how you'd react."

"He robbed a liquor store," I said. "Everybody deserves second chances."

Barack shook his head. "There's more to the story. He killed the shopkeeper. Jenkins Brown was only fourteen at the time, but he was tried as an adult. He pled guilty to first-degree manslaughter — a plea deal for turning on his accomplices. They're still in prison, but Jenkins is a free man."

My thumb hesitated on the CALL button. No wonder Shaun's aunt was worried about her nephew getting too involved with the Red Door. I wouldn't want my family getting in bed with murderers either, no matter how "reformed" they were.

I also knew it wasn't my place to judge.

Jenkins Brown had done his time. He'd served his debt to society. What he did was, ultimately, between him and God. And if you wanted to catch a killer, sometimes you had to work with one.

What really disturbed me was that I was already thinking of Shaun's shooter as a killer, even though Shaun was, far as we knew, on the road to recovery. The more of the city I saw, the more I felt hope slipping away.

32

Steve picked us up. I got into the passenger seat. It appeared that he'd recovered miraculously. "You OK to be driving, Steve?" I asked. "You're not gonna faint again?"

"It was an act, Joe," Barack said.

"What?"

"Steve 'fainted' to let me give him the slip," Barack explained. "Not his fault if he faints. Can't get in trouble with the boss for fainting."

"Ah, nice," I said, then slapped Steve on the arm. "You're not as much of a snowflake as I thought, kid. You enjoy the birch massage?"

Steve gripped the steering wheel. "I'm not ready to talk about that yet."

We rode in silence on the southbound freeway. I wanted to turn the radio on — anything to drown out the silence — but I'd already laid down the law regarding music in a man's automobile. If there's one thing

Joe Biden ain't, it's a hypocrite.

I glanced at Barack in the backseat. He was getting in a little shuteye. I was too keyed up to fall asleep. I was running on adrenaline at this point. It reminded me of the all-nighters we used to pull in the Senate. All I had to do was keep it together for a few more hours. Once we talked to the pastor, I'd have a better idea how long I was going to need to stay in town. Jill would understand, once she heard the full story.

Steve's phone rang and he answered it on his Bluetooth.

Yeah . . . Uh-huh . . . OK . . .

He finished and turned to me. "They traced the plates of the car that almost took you guys out in the parking garage," he said. "A couple of agents went to talk to the owner. Said the car had been parked on the street all morning as far as he knew, so they're treating it as a stolen vehicle. There's an APB out for it. Sounds like somebody was driving it like a nut because it was hot."

Steve's news didn't make me feel any better or put an end to my creeping paranoia. Somebody didn't want us looking into this shooting. I already knew one of those somebodies was Rahm, but he wouldn't send someone to run us down. I didn't even think Bento Box would go out of his way to do that. You'd have to be pretty stupid to target a former president and vice president. Stupid, or desperate. When it came to criminals, though, they were all either stupid, desperate, or some combination of both.

Which category had Pastor Brown fallen into when he'd been sent to the big house as a teenager? I replayed everything he'd said to me in Shaun's hospital room. He hadn't exactly lied about what he'd done, but he hadn't been forthcoming about it, either. Then again, I wouldn't expect somebody who'd taken another person's life to be forthcoming unless pressed, especially if they'd done their time and found salvation.

Fourteen-year-old Jenkins Brown had been tried as an adult. That didn't make him an adult when he pulled the trigger. Barack explained that the accomplices had been eighteen and nineteen, and although Brown was the one who pulled the trigger, they were the ones who bore the brunt of the punishment. Neither cut a plea deal. Brown testified at their separate trials. Threats had been made against him, and there were stories of hit jobs foiled in lockup. The two other men, now approaching fifty, wouldn't be eligible for parole until they were older than I was now.

Barack knew all of this.

There was no single victim. There was the shopkeeper, who had lost his life. There were also his three children, who had been robbed of their father. But hadn't Brown and his accomplices also been robbed of their innocence, years before they became criminals? Society had let them down. Whose fault was that? Who took the blame for a fourteen-year-old kid running the streets without supervision, sticking up liquor stores?

There were no easy answers. Even the questions were difficult.

33

We parked in front of the Red Door, near where Michelle had dropped me off. It reminded me that I hadn't told Barack that his wife had given me a ride. He wouldn't have minded, but I couldn't very well bring it up *now* — A) it would seem suspicious that I hadn't mentioned it earlier, and B) he would quickly suss out the real reason I hadn't told him (i.e., that I'd suspected Pastor Brown and his flock had some involvement in the shooting at the freight yard). Learning about the Crooks had eliminated most of my suspicions, but I didn't want Barack to think I was going around checking up on his friends.

Steve went to plug the meter.

"It's not working," I said.

He turned back to me.

"It looks like it's out of order," I said. "The little thing with the . . . never mind."

He slapped the meter a couple of times,

trying to get it to work. Every one on the block — broken on purpose, I suspected. "Free" parking for the Red Door, courtesy of the City Streets Department. Steve eyed me with suspicion. The only way I could have known about the meter was if I'd been down here already. Thankfully, Barack was busy backing out of the car, unfolding himself onto the sidewalk with great care.

"The meter's broken," Steve said to Barack. "Do you think they'll tow my car?"

"I wouldn't worry . . . too much."

Steve looked like he was about to tear up. This had not been a great day for him — but, to be fair, we'd all had a pretty stressful day. We'd been bouncing around the city for what felt like a three-day weekend. It was hard to believe I'd landed just that morning.

Barack went straight to the red door, which to my surprise was unlocked. Perhaps I should have expected it, seeing as how Pastor Brown had told us he'd meet us here. But still.

"Everything OK, Joe?" Barack asked, holding it open for me.

Inside, a young man greeted us and told us to wait in the lobby. I could hear sounds coming from the main chapel. One of the doors was open a smidge. I peeked in. An auditorium, with hundreds of empty seats. The lights were up and a gospel choir was practicing. I wondered how many of the young adults onstage had criminal records.

I felt ashamed that was the first thing that had come to mind.

Barack joined me at the chapel door. "Thinking about joining? I'm sure they could use another baritone."

We listened to the choir run through "Tell It," a gospel track I hadn't heard in some years. Even with the frequent starts and stops, they were knocking it out of the park. They didn't need Joe Biden's raspy wind-pipes.

"You know this one?" Barack asked.

I realized my foot was tapping along. "This might come as a shock, but I've been to a few black churches in my day. And not just for campaign stops."

He nodded. Under the harsh hallway lighting, he looked much older than his age. It wasn't just the gray hair. It was every-thing. What did my weathered mug look like right now? On good days, the years lined my face like growth rings on a tree. The only comfort was that I wouldn't be the oldest bag of bones running for president. Bernie had already entered the race, taking that dubious honor.

"The trouble is kids think they're going to live forever," I said. "Lord knows I was a hellion at their age, but I wasn't running around robbing freight yards and shooting off pistols."

"Maybe they know they're not going to live forever. What have they got to lose?"

I turned to him. "A lot. I've been living on borrowed time most of my adult life. I've had two aneurysms. I looked Death in the face and told him to scram. Look at everything I've accomplished since then."

"Think about it from these kids' perspective, Joe. They're living in a violent world. They know that any day they wake up could be their last. It's not the life they chose to lead."

"But nobody forces them into gangs."

"What's the alternative? We have twenty kids in Rising Stars now, all from Chicago. All paid for by Caruso, who even takes the time to do some of the mentoring himself. I'm sure he had other things to do today besides visit one of his kids in the hospital. I don't know if you saw how many applications we had when you were in the records room, but it was over three thousand. For twenty openings. They need after-school programs. Jobs. But what do they get? A little religion? I wish it were enough."

I shook my head. Crime and poverty went together like peanut butter and jelly. It was a situation even the best of kids couldn't pull themselves out of. Not without help. It also wasn't a problem that the country could arrest its way out of. We'd already tried that.

Barack nodded along with the choir.

"It doesn't mean Michelle and I won't keep trying to reach these kids," he said. "They just need some help seeing that they have futures. That's why we're building the community center on the South Side. They need hope."

Hope. It had been a while since I'd heard that word come out of Barack's mouth with such conviction. Now I just needed to believe in it again myself.

34

The pastor listened to our story, nodding his head as Barack laid out our hypothesis: find the thieves, find the shooter. He didn't seem surprised in the slightest that we'd come to see him for help with the Crooks. In fact, he seemed to take it as a source of pride.

"They're one of the gangs we have to deal with from time to time," he said, leaning back in his plush chair. We were in his office, which was adorned with paintings of Martin Luther King Jr. and a dark-skinned Jesus. "I've had to step in between the gangs to negotiate ceasefires when things get out of control. Gang wars aren't good for anybody: the gangs, the neighborhood. Nobody."

"I'm sorry," I cut in. "You know who the gang members are, you know the leaders. They're selling drugs on the streets, in your neighborhood. Why don't you go to the cops?"

Pastor Brown scrunched up his face like I'd just called Mike Pence a decent guy. "You remember the War on Drugs? You know who won, right?" He paused, but not long enough for me to respond. "*The drugs.* The losers were the addicts — their families, their friends. We were all losers."

What he was saying was true, but it didn't mean I had to accept it. There were other ways to live. Giving up and letting gangs control your neighborhood without any resistance? I didn't like it.

"What do you think would happen if the police grew a pair and arrested every gang member?" he continued. "I'll tell you: another gang would move in. Because the customers are here. People like to get high. Especially when they don't have anything else. Unemployment around here is close to fifty percent. That hasn't changed in generations. I wish it weren't the case, but I'm a realist."

Barack looked like he wanted to say something, but he kept his mouth shut. He'd been a community organizer on these same streets. If anyone knew what Pastor Brown was up against, it was Barack Obama.

"The Church used to say drugs were tools of the devil," I said. "You don't see the devil's handiwork when you look around and all you see is broken lives?"

"If by 'the devil' you mean 'the white man,' then I definitely see his handiwork. I see it all over. But if you're asking about Satan — the great deceiver — I've got news for you, friend: the fire and brimstone days of preaching are long gone, at least around these parts. Ain't nobody got time for the devil. We got too many man-made problems to be worried about him."

"Can you help us?" Barack asked.

"Help you, or help Shaun? I'll do what I can. I hear you all put some extra security up in St. Bernard's."

"We thought whoever shot him might return to finish the job," I said. "You don't think it's necessary?"

Pastor Brown shrugged. "I could tell you that gangbangers don't go around shooting up hospitals, but it happens. I'm asking because as soon as word gets around that there are Feds in town, nobody's going to want to talk. Mouths are going to shut up, and fast."

"It's just us," Barack said. "And Steve."

Steve, standing near the door, didn't say anything.

"There are three reasons you get shot in the hood," Pastor Brown said. "One, drugs are involved. Buying, selling, that sort of thing. Miscommunication, robbery. Two, you're messing around with somebody's girl. Don't do it."

"And the other reason?" I said.

"Racist-ass cops."

The clerk whom the pastor had shot in cold blood hadn't been involved in the drug trade, and he hadn't been hitting on anyone's girlfriend, as far as I knew. He'd simply been doing his job.

I could tell by Barack's narrowed eyes that he was thinking along the same lines, that perhaps Pastor Brown wasn't being quite as forthcoming as he seemed.

Still, I believed Pastor Brown when he said he would do what he could. He didn't know why Shaun had been shot — none of the kids who knew Shaun through the Red Door had heard rumblings of him messing around with a gang member's girl, as far as the pastor knew. They insisted that Shaun wasn't into drugs — not cocaine, not crack, not heroin, not pills. Drinking a little, here and there. The idea that Shaun would help anyone — especially a gang like the Crooks — steal a shipment of guns was the most ridiculous assertion of all, Pastor Brown said. Shaun's mother had lost her life in the crossfire of a shootout. Whatever Shaun's rap sheet looked like, he'd never so much as touched a gun.

I wondered if Barack and I should maybe talk to some of these kids — presumably, a few were in the choir rehearsing in the auditorium. But I didn't think I could get any of them to talk to me. If they weren't willing to confess to Pastor Brown, then they weren't going to let anything slip to me. I imagined they'd be too star-struck to talk to Barack. I would be if I was them.

We didn't have a motive for the shooting yet, which still distressed me. Pastor Brown assured me we'd find one once we found the shooter.

"If you will excuse me now, I'll make some phone calls and see if we can't get this resolved," he said.

We stepped outside. I turned to Barack. "Doesn't this make you nervous? That this supposed community leader has gang lords on speed dial?"

"Stop and reflect for a minute, Joe. What is it you think I did as a community organizer? I fought for change, acting as a liaison between the neighborhood and City Hall. When you're involved in the community, you need to reach out to all parties. Sometimes, that means talking to gangs; some-times, it means talking to the police. It may look like a war zone from the outside, but if you know the rules, you're a lot less likely than you'd think to get shot."

"That's what's bugging me. Every indication is that Shaun knew the rules."

"Maybe he made a mistake. He seems like a strong-willed kid, though. Don't count him out. It's like Hemingway said: The world breaks us all, but we become stronger in those broken places."

"I wish he wasn't alone," I said.

"His mother's still with him," Barack said, tapping his temple. "Inside here. Those voices . . . the ones that shape you . . . you can't ever shake them from your head."

I nodded. "Like ghosts."

We stood in the hallway in silence, but for the heavenly sounds of the young men's voices singing in the choir.

35

"Did either of you see a restroom around here?" I asked, stretching. We were still waiting for Pastor Brown to emerge from his office.

Steve pointed down the hall. "Around the corner, then to your left."

"You been here before or something?"

"It was on the fire-exit map when we first came in."

Steve was observant, I'd give him that much. He was also undersized, so you couldn't duck behind him in a crisis. A good agent, though. I'd never believed he would last long on the Counter-Assault Team, no matter which president he was working for. Sure, you got to dress up like a SWAT-team member and carry heavy military artillery around, but you spent your life riding in the back of a black van, trailing the president's motorcade from city to city. That had to be hot as a Russian sauna. Steve sweated enough as it was. He was born with overactive sweat glands, he'd told me once. I'd seen a commercial on TV for sweat gland laser surgery, where they zap them and then you don't sweat anymore. Ever. Something about it didn't sound safe to me, and when I mentioned it to Steve, he said that he knew someone who'd had it done and good golly, Miss Molly, *it worked* . . . but the sweat still had to get out of your body somehow, some way, and this poor fellow started to sweat from his forehead and his butt cheeks. I noticed at that moment several perspiration beads forming on Steve's forehead. He'd been talking about himself. Which made it all the more heroic he'd agreed to wear his suit into the sauna and put on a show pretending to overheat.

Inside the men's room there were three stalls and two urinals — a tall one for men, a shorter one for boys (or Steve). I was all alone. Good. I'd heard horror stories from Barack about autograph hounds in public restrooms. I'd never been approached in one, which I assumed was because I used a very defensive posture at urinals. A wide stance, like a cowboy who'd been riding a horse for three days. I'd been told my stance was very intimidating, and that was how I liked it.

I didn't need a urinal today. I entered the first stall and closed the door.

I didn't take my time, but I wasn't quick about my business, either. Pastor Brown was making us wait, and we'd still be waiting, I guessed, no matter how long I took. I wanted to see this thing through — the whole nasty business with Shaun and the Crooks — but it was time to be realistic about the situation. How long was I willing to hang out in Chicago?

There was no shame in heading home after giving it my all. I was a fighter, but I was no dummy. I had decisions to make about the country. About my family. A dark part of me wondered if I wasn't running away from those decisions by refusing to leave until I'd personally seen justice prevail.

As I washed up, I refused to meet my own eyes in the mirror. How could I even think such thoughts? Shaun wasn't some stall tactic. He was a kid. The real reason why I was rethinking staying in town was because I was scared — scared of what I would do with all the anger coursing through me.

If Pastor Brown found Shaun's shooter, I prayed that he turned the suspect shooter over to the police before we got a look at him. Because I was afraid I might take a swing at him, and another, and another, until either my fists gave out or his face did. My bones might have been old, but they'd been hardened, not weakened, by the years. The skin on my knuckles was tough as leather.

On my way out of the restroom, I felt a draft coming through a door that had been left propped open. Inside, I could see a warehouse stocked with boxes. At the far end, a garage door was open — the loading dock. The air outdoors was cooling down now that the sun had set. What was the heating bill on a place this size? They must have had some sizable donations coming in. Not that it was any of my business. The Catholic Church wasn't exactly known for its fiscal conservatism.

I couldn't stand to see doors left open like that. I used to harp on it at home with my kids, and at work with the vice-presidential residence staff. Leave a door open and you were burning money by the handful. Besides, hadn't our poor environment been through enough? We owed it to future generations to make wiser choices about energy usage. This was their planet, not ours.

The argument worked better on staff than on teenagers.

I poked my head out the garage door to

see if anyone was around. The moving truck was parked against a far wall, underneath a carport, alongside three white vans — the kind used by contractors and churches everywhere, the kind of vans that were so ubiquitous and anonymous they often sat in plain sight on streets without being noticed. I'd heard one story of a cable technician who had died at the wheel in a van like that parked on the streets of Midtown Manhattan. It took three full days before somebody noticed his slumped body and called the cops, by which time the guy was stiff as a two-by-four.

I almost hit the garage door button but decided I'd let the pastor know that someone had left the barn door wide open. Not my circus.

On my way back, I took a closer look at the boxes. I truly didn't think they were filled with anything more than canned goods from a food drive, but I couldn't resist taking a peek.

There were Patriot shipping labels attached to the sides and tops of every box, with the addresses blacked out in marker.

I didn't know which containers had been robbed at the freight yard, but I remembered seeing that same eagle logo. The eagle looked more like Delaware's state bird, the blue hen, but then again I was no art aficionado. The real question was whether the boxes were from the same shipping containers that I'd seen at Norfolk Southern. If they were, it would go a long ways toward explaining how the police knew who had hit the freight yard, but Pastor Brown — buddy-buddy with the local gangs — supposedly hadn't heard a peep.

I knew what Pa Biden would have said: *Only blind men believe in coincidences. The rest of us can see the connections. If you don't, it's because you're not looking hard enough.*

I'd asked if he knew anyone who was blind, and he said he'd known a few umpires back in the day.

That was Pa Biden for you.

I backed up slowly into the hallway . . . and ran smack dab into Pastor Brown.

36

Barack and Steve exited the men's room to see the pastor and me engaged in an epic staredown in the warehouse doorway.

"I was wondering where you'd gone off to," Barack said. "Thought you might have fallen in."

Steve winced for some reason.

"I didn't fall in," I said. "I just got lost on my way back. You OK, Steve?"

"Touchy subject," Barack said. "Steve here was a well baby, you know."

Steve's face flushed red. "Please, Mr. President, I'd rather not talk about it."

"Oh, come on," Barack said. "You fell down a well when you were, what, three?"

"Twelve," Steve said.

"Little old for a well baby," I said. "Who was the big one? Back in '87? Baby Jessica. I had just declared my first presidential run and was nearly eclipsed by her news coverage. You ever meet her?"

"Of course," Steve said. "There's a whole convention circuit. Me, Baby Jessica. The spooky girl from *The Ring*."

Pastor Brown ignored our tomfoolery. He was still staring through me. I hadn't been lost, and he knew it. However, he didn't know what I had or hadn't seen while snooping in the warehouse. I had my suspicions, but that was it. If I held my tongue until later, when I could discuss things with Barack, there was a chance that the boxes would be cleared out. If there was anything incriminating in them, it would be long gone by the time we returned.

A big "if." Did I want to stake my friendship with Barack on a suspicious feeling?

This isn't about you and him.

This is about justice.

"Were you looking for something, Mr. Biden?" the pastor asked. An electric charge passed between us. I wasn't the only one who felt it. I could see Steve's nostrils flare, which was this little thing he did when he tensed up.

"If you were looking for the vending machines, I'm sure we can pick up some Gatorade en route to the Tribune Tower," Barack said. "Unless, of course, you'd rather head home. Your call."

"What about the Crooks?" I asked.

"We've got that all under control," Pastor Brown said.

Barack put a hand on my shoulder. "The pastor has a meeting set up next week with the gang leadership and a couple representatives from the Chicago PD. He's going to mediate, see if he can't negotiate a settlement between the two sides."

I shrugged off his hand. "Do the Crooks know who shot Shaun? If they do, they need to turn him over. Screw this 'negotiating.' "

"It's not that easy," the pastor said. "You think they'll give up his name without getting something in return? That might be how you do things in your neck of the woods, but this is Chicago."

I didn't like him suggesting that I didn't know what was going on in my own backyard. I'd seen corruption; I'd flushed it out. And I'd keep fighting it until all the fight in me was gone.

Barack could see that I was seething below the surface. He stepped between Pastor Brown and me to create some space for us to simmer. Steve, drawing on years of Secret Service training and experience, pulled Barack back. He wasn't going to let an errant punch land on his protectee. I hadn't thought it was possible to move Barack like that, but Steve was, pound for pound, a tough little *hombre.*

So was I.

Pastor Brown outweighed me by a hundred pounds. Easily. I'd taken on bullies his size back when I was a scrawny middle schooler and won. Ma Biden had a rule: if you lose a fight, don't come home and expect dinner. Dinner is for winners.

"You know what I think?" I said. "I think you know a lot more about this shooting than you're letting on."

"President Obama, Barry, take your boy here home. He's drunk."

"I've never had a drink in my life," I said, pointing an indignant finger at him.

"Joe," Barack said.

"What?" I growled back, not taking my eyes off Pastor Brown.

"It's time to go. It's been a long day for all of us. And to be fair to Pastor Brown, you and I don't know Chicago like he does. I've been gone a long time. Neighborhoods change; people change. Some things, however, remain the same. This is a dangerous town. It's gotten better, but it's no Mayberry. Even if we solve this case, it won't stem the flow of guns into the city. It'll ease our minds, but not a damn thing more." There was straight fire behind the president's speech this time. "You can't fix things in a day, or a month, or a year. We can't take our frustrations out on this man or his church. Don't take it out on the people who are fighting for the same thing we're fighting for."

I shook my head. "You think he's fighting for the same thing? He's got you fooled. He's got everyone fooled. But I see what's really going on."

"You're not making sense," Barack said.

"I'll show you. See those?" I gestured toward the boxes stacked three shelves high. There had to be forty or fifty boxes, all with the Patriot shipping logo. That stupid flipping bird. "Why don't you ask the pastor what's in those boxes, huh? Go ahead. I'll wait."

Barack sighed. He pressed his long fingers to his graying temples. "I don't see what —"

"Ask him."

Barack turned to Pastor Brown. "I apologize for this. But I've known Joe a long time, and if he's sure of something, well, he's a pit bull. He sinks his teeth in and won't let go." He looked at me. "And he's always correct. Isn't that right, Joe?"

I nodded.

"By that same token, I've known you a long time, Pastor," he said. "And I've never had a reason to distrust you, either. You have to understand the situation this puts me in."

Pastor Brown nodded solemnly. "Not everyone approves of the way I do business. I'm making do with what I have to work with. It's a miracle that we're able to keep our lights on. It's only through the grace of God —"

"Aw, hell with it," I said, making a dash for the closest stack of boxes. The pastor tried to lay a hand on me, but he was no match for Joe Biden's fleet feet. I slipped out of range, feeling his fingers brush within an inch of my jacket. In record time, I was ripping at packing tape, pulling up flaps in a flurry. I was vaguely aware of voices — yelling, shouting my name — but I was a man possessed.

I tore into the cardboard like a kid trying to get at the prize inside a box of Cracker Jacks. It was time to rip the mask off this Scooby-Doo villain and expose him to the world. Unfortunately, what I found inside the box was even more disappointing than a Cracker Jack temporary tattoo of that sailor kid and his dog.

37

"Beans."

I pulled a can from the box and examined the label. Bush's Baked Beans. Original flavor.

"Beans?" Barack said. "I'm not sure I understand, Joe."

I didn't understand either. I set the can down and hauled out another two, three more. I peeled up the cardboard separating them from . . . more beans. Beans, beans, beans, all the way to the bottom. Bush's happened to be my go-to for family picnics, but that didn't help with my confusion. I'd been so sure. Or had I? Had I let Barack and the pastor back me into a corner, and then come up with this show as a last-ditch bid to make some sort of difference? My mind was clouded with doubt and second-guessing.

It wasn't the Biden way.

Wait. They hit three different shipping

containers at the freight yard. Wasn't that what the Record Store guy had said? *They were amateurs. They weren't expecting to find the guns . . .*

I tore into another box like it was a Christmas present. Except there weren't baked beans in this box. There were peas. Canned peas, in all their foul, salty, gray-green glory.

This was the worst Christmas ever.

"Mr. Biden?" Steve said. "Maybe you should —"

"Shut it, Well Baby," I said, and kept tearing into boxes in such a frenzy that nobody could stop me for fear of getting torn up themselves. The shouting stopped, and, after ripping up half a dozen boxes and finding nothing but canned food, I realized a chilling silence had fallen over the room.

All eyes were on me.

"They . . . there were three containers, you see? Two had . . . I don't know what they had . . . could have been canned food . . . could have . . ."

I fell flat on my ass. My shoulders slumped.

"I'm not sure what you thought you were going to find," Barack said, picking up one of the cans. He read the label with a mixture of amusement and sadness.

"I have an idea," Pastor Brown said.

We all looked at him. I shook my head. *Don't say it, don't say it . . .*

"He thought I'd jacked those guns. All we got here is a good ol'-fashioned food drive. My guys pick up donations from grocery stores all over the city — some of the food is expired, some of the cans are dented, but that don't matter to the people we distribute to. We're feeding more families in this community than any welfare program, believe that."

"You're saying Joe thought you were mixed up with this gun business?" Barack turned to me. "Tell me he's wrong, Joe."

I didn't say anything. Barack understood. In that moment, he understood. The look of disappointment on his face was one I'd seen a time or two before. It wasn't one I'd ever wanted to see again.

"I don't know what I was thinking," I said. I wouldn't have bought my line, but it was true. I bumbled through a long, rambling excuse that may or may not have hit the following bullet points: *My thoughts were all jumbled up. I'd been on the road too long. I was exhausted. I was half certain, at one point during the day, that an actual leprechaun was following me. I hadn't had my afternoon nap, or my early evening nap. I didn't remember*

241

the last thing I had to eat. Was I suffering the effects of low blood sugar? The pastor was angry when he left the forum, he'd said it was because he wanted to find a real breakfast, not bagels but chicken and waffles, and it sounded like a phony story because who doesn't like bagels, and —

"Stop, Joe." Barack shook his head. "We can talk about this tomorrow, after you've had a good, long sleep." He took Pastor Brown off to the side to have a few words in private. They spoke in hushed tones, throwing a glance my way every so often.

Steve kneeled beside me. "Can I get you something? A glass of water? A Xanax?"

"A cab," I said, and left it at that. When my ride showed up, I slipped away without saying another word to anyone. Barack was still busy trying to appease Pastor Brown and wasn't paying attention to me anyway. Besides, the more I talked, the deeper the hole I would dig. The time had come, at long last, to shut my big mouth.

38

The cab dropped me off at the other end of the terminal from Delta. A slow rain had begun to fall. I hoofed it the two hundred yards in the elements. I could have gotten out of the rain inside, but it didn't feel right. A little rain to wash away the sins felt like a small penance, but a penance nonetheless.

As I was about to enter the terminal, a man with a heavy Chicago accent shouted my name.

I fixed a phony smile on my face and turned. I wasn't in the mood for taking a selfie, but I'd sign the guy's ticket. Or whatever else he wanted. As long as he had a Sharpie. I didn't have one, and I wasn't going to wait around forever to find one.

I wasn't expecting to recognize him.

A man in a Bears jacket — the all-meat-and-no-potatoes cabbie who'd picked me up that morning at arrivals — skidded to a stop in his Air Jordans just inches from colliding with me. He must have been parked in the long line of taxis and seen me walking by. It was dark out now, but apparently not dark enough.

"I thought it was you," he said. He sniffled, then spit a huge loogie into the street. "Sorry about that. Getting over a cold. You know how it is."

I didn't have the luxury of getting sick these days, but I didn't say that. Instead, I thanked him for the ride earlier in the day and said, "Got a plane to catch, though, so if you'll excuse me . . ."

"Just a minute." He reached inside his jacket, sending a shiver up my spine. What if he was a wacko? You couldn't tell these days — there seemed to be more and more of them around, emboldened by the current political climate to let their abhorrent freak flags fly. The stuff people did and said in public anymore blew my mind. Sooner or later, somebody was going to take the partisan rhetoric too far. Sooner or later, somebody was going to get hurt.

I watched his hand as it emerged. We were close enough that if he pulled a weapon, I could lower my shoulder and lean into him — take him to the ground and then wrestle his gun or knife away.

"You left this in my cab," he said.

Murder on the Amtrak Express.

I breathed a sigh of relief.

I'd forgotten all about the damned book.

"Keep it," I said.

His face fell. "Ya don't want it?"

"I've read it. What's it going to do, sit there on my bookshelf? Books are meant to be passed around, like a girly mag in middle school."

"Gee, I never thought of it that way, Mr. Biden."

Anticipating his next question — and in the interest of expediting our entire awkward interaction — I asked if he wanted me to sign the book for him.

He puckered his lips in an odd way, which I realized must have been him trying to shake off the raindrops that had accumulated on his thick mustache. "You didn't write it, though."

I laughed. "I didn't, but I thought you might like a souvenir. You never know if the guy you're talking to could be, say, the next president of the United States."

Now he was intrigued. "Wait a minute. Are you suggesting . . ."

I gave him a wink.

"When you put it that way, all right," he said, handing me the book. It was getting pelted by the rain, which was falling harder and harder by the minute. Though the sky was black as midnight, I imagined great Midwestern storm clouds overhead. Perhaps the storm would cool things off a bit, wash the blood from the streets.

I tucked the paperback under my arm to keep it dry while Ditka searched his pockets for a pen. My phone rang. I ignored it at first but, sensing my new friend wasn't going to find a writing implement anytime soon, answered the call on the third ring. It was Steve.

"Talk to me," I said.

"We found him. The shooter."

"That was fast."

"No kidding," he said. "We had that APB out for the stolen BMW coupe that almost ran you and Renegade down, right? The cops spotted it on the Dan Ryan, heading out of town. There was a chase. Nobody was hurt — well, nobody but the driver."

"They think he was the shooter?" I couldn't believe it. The second I stepped away from the case, they solved it.

"The driver was an eighteen-year-old kid. Kendrick Jackson. A Crook. They found the stolen gun in the glove box. My guess is his prints will be all over it."

Ditka held up a finger and ran back to his cab. Going for a pen.

"You have a motive?" I asked. "What about the president's BlackBerry?"

Negative on the BlackBerry, Steve said. The motive, meanwhile, could have been an argument about sports scores, for all anyone knew. The crash had killed him on impact. Young gang members were full of testosterone, with too much free time. The detectives would be interviewing the suspect's friends, who were mostly gang members as well. The gang leadership wanted this over and done with. The kid had been a loose cannon. They promised to cooperate with the police. It struck me as funny — not funny "ha-ha" but funny "weird." Gangs, police, churches. All on the same side.

Whether it was the side of good or evil was still up in the air.

I sighed, having had enough of all this talk. "Is President Obama there?"

There was a short silence on the other end. "You're going to need to give him some time."

This wasn't my first stint in the doghouse. Back when I was veep I'd come out for gay marriage before him, which ticked him off since he'd been planning to do it first. I'd jumped the gun, bungling the rollout of our administration's support of a key issue, but I'd been in the right. Barack eventually saw that I'd meant well.

This time was different. Even if I'd meant well, this wasn't a case of me saying the wrong thing at the wrong time. This wasn't a classic "Biden-ism." It was a cock-up, plain and simple.

"Thanks, Steve. I understand."

"Goodbye, Mr. Biden."

"Before you go, I'm sorry I called you Well Baby. And Snowflake."

"It's OK," he said. "I've been called worse."

"About the birch massage . . ."

"I'm still not ready to talk about that."

Ditka and I took shelter under an outcropping. He handed me his pen. It was shaped like a baseball bat, complete with a Cubs logo. Nice rubber grip. Total crap for writing.

"Got it at a Cubs game for filling out my scorecard," he said as I scrawled my name in the book. "Usually you do that with pencils, but it was three bucks and . . . Why do we fill out scorecards anyways? They got all the stats on the internets now. Da computers. I don't know why I do it, must be cuz my dad used to take me to Wrigley when I was a kid. But oh, back then, you could sit in the bleachers for five bucks. It was no place for children, though — I seen some stuff there that you wouldn't believe. Or maybe you would . . ."

His voice faded into the background as a thunderclap struck. He paid it no mind — just kept jawing away like he'd been sent from the heavens with the express purpose of making me miss my flight. But nothing was going to make me do that. Not Ditka here, and not a little rain. I was getting on that plane and we were taking off, even if I had to fly it myself.

39

The flight attendant welcomed me aboard with a smile as forced as my own. He was a young man, right out of high school or college, with a frosted sheath of hair that sat atop his head like a glacier. He asked if I had any bags.

"Only the ones under my eyes," I said. The Chicago detour was just a day trip, so my luggage had been sent home. with my tour manager. My clothes were waiting for me back in Wilmington right now.

So was my family.

I took my seat in first class. Plane fares were coming out of my own pocket these days, not the taxpayers'. Nobody was going to tell me I hadn't earned it.

"Looks like it's just us," the attendant said. I was the only first-class passenger onboard. "What would you like to drink?"

"Diet Coke," I said. "And peanuts."

"Would you like a wineglass for your Coke?"

I stared at him for a beat.

"Kidding," he said. "I'll be right back."

I could have done a little finger-gun in his direction to let him know I wasn't pissed, but I *was* pissed. Not at him. Not at anyone besides myself. I should have been in a better mood. Barack and I had done everything we'd set out to do: we'd helped track down Shaun Denton's shooter. What bothered me was everything else that had transpired between us. Not only the part in the last couple of hours. It was everything, going back a week, to when he first phoned me.

Barack thought he was doing me a favor by inviting me to meet his pal Caruso. I appreciated it, but it had felt forced from the beginning. A blind date. If only I'd been upfront with Barack about the elephant in the room — or in this case, the donkey. Despite all the time I'd spent teasing a third run for president, I was still only ninety-five percent there. (This was up from ninety percent a few months back.) I hadn't discussed my plans — or lack thereof — with Barack recently. I didn't have to. He knew, perhaps better than anyone, what the internal debate in my head sounded like. The never-ending book tour had been a success, but it paled in comparison to the road ahead. Even as the frontrunner, I would have to fight my own party; if I passed that test, I would graduate to the general election. No matter how much money I raised or endorsements I bagged, it was going to be a long uphill slog.

To paraphrase Barack, hard things were hard.

The plane started backing up. A female flight attendant who sounded like Lindsey Graham (and, poor girl, looked like Lindsey Graham) was leading the passengers through instructions for buckling their seatbelts.

The first-class attendant handed me my drink in a plastic cup. There was a lot of ice in it. It was more like ice with a splash of Diet Coke.

Just the way I liked it.

We waited in line on the taxiway. I wondered what it would be like to fly a plane. Flying planes was one activity I had never gotten into. It wasn't a hobby. There was no place for amateurs.

One could say the same for detective work.

Not that Barack and I had done too bad a job. We'd had a little help from the Secret Service — Steve might get a nod in the acknowledgments if this were a book — but we'd done a lot of the legwork ourselves. Tonight, I would sleep well knowing that I'd done some good. If it all left a bad taste in my mouth, it was because of my own actions. At least I could say that justice had been served. The shooter was on his way to the morgue, once they scraped what was left of him off the interstate. Frontier justice, of a grim variety.

We weren't in the air yet. I decided to take a quick peek at Barack's Instagram to see if he'd posted anything from the VIP event. Had Caruso shown up? Was Oprah there, schmoozing potential donors?

Nothing from tonight. The last post was of him, Pastor Brown, and Caruso. Taken this morning before the prayer breakfast. The three of them were laughing. About what, I wondered. About Amtrak Joe, the delusional old man who thought he had a chance at the presidency? *He'd be forty thousand years old by the time of his inauguration!*

The joke was on them. The first time I'd run for Senate, I hadn't been old enough to take office until after the election. Everyone had laughed then, too. I'd proved them all wrong. I could do it again.

If I wanted to.

Something about Barack's post was nagging me. I finally realized what it was: Caruso's checkered suit jacket. Almost as ugly as Barack's tan abomination. It had been hanging in the green room. The phone in Caruso's jacket had buzzed while I was in the room with Barack this morning.

It's not mine, Barack had told me. *I already checked.*

Maybe Barack's BlackBerry wasn't stolen.

Maybe another BlackBerry user had mistakenly picked up the wrong phone.

Maybe Caruso wasn't as retired from the gang lifestyle as he boasted.

What sealed the deal for me were his knuckle tattoos, which I hadn't seen clearly enough to read when I'd met him earlier. C-R-O-O-K-L-Y-F. Crook life. Barack had to have known that Caruso was a former Crook. Caruso was supposed to meet me at the forum, but had left around the time of the shooting. He was Shaun's mentor, so he would have known where the kid worked and what his schedule was. I could see the rapper ducking through the rusted-out fencing at the freight yard and waiting for Shaun to show up. Maybe the Crook, Kendrick, pulled the trigger; maybe Caruso gave Kendrick the gun to dispose of afterward.

I phoned Steve. He answered with a

grumble. "Shouldn't you be on a plane right now?"

"Steve, I need your help."

I was hunched over in my seat, trying to avoid the nasty looks the frosted-hair attendant was shooting my way. *I know I'm not supposed to be on the phone, but chill out. We're taxiing. We could be doing this for another hour.*

"This will have to wait," Steve said. "We've got a big event here, and there are a lot of moving pieces. I've got to go."

"I have an idea. I need somebody to check it out. That's all I'm asking. There was a jacket in the green room today. A checkered jacket —"

"They took the green room apart. It's a conference room again. There's nothing down there. No jackets, nothing."

"Is he there?" I asked.

"Who, Barack?"

"Caruso."

There was a heavy sigh on the other end. "He's here, but —"

"It's him! Don't you see? It's —"

"Goodbye, Joe."

The line went dead. I called back and went straight to voicemail. His mailbox was full. Steve thought I was losing it. There was talk that, if I was elected president, I'd be the oldest president in history. Facts are facts, but mentally I was sharp as the reaper's sickle. I was playing with a full deck, and screw anyone who thought otherwise.

"We need to turn this plane around," I announced.

40

The first-class flight attendant was staring at me in shock. He was strapped into a seat outside the cockpit, belts crisscrossing his upper body so that he didn't tumble down the aisle if the plane stopped abruptly.

"We need to turn around," I said, louder this time. "Get ahold of the captain. If we don't turn around, by God, somebody is going to die."

The runway was going past us in a blur.

"That came out wrong," I said, realizing my verbal gaffe. "I'm not a hijacker."

The roar of the engine was so loud that I worried my voice was drowned out. By the look on the flight attendant's face, all he'd heard was "hijacker."

It was a classic Biden-ism, but nobody was laughing.

The attendant picked up the phone to relay something to the cockpit. What in tarnation had I done? My heart was beating fast, like I had a racehorse in my chest *ka-thump*ing down the final stretch of the Kentucky Derby, a pint-sized jockey on its back holding on for dear life. If we did turn around, I'd be handcuffed, dragged kicking and screaming to Cook County Jail.

The cabin lights flickered. The engines seemed to cut out, too, as the brakes locked up. The flight attendant tipped forward, the phone tumbling from his hands. I gripped the armrests tight as the wheels screeched and we skidded toward the end of the runway. Beyond lay a fence, and then a cluster of trees, a little forest. On the other side of that, head- and taillights, a four-lane highway.

My status as the presumed frontrunner for the Democratic presidential nomination was about to go up in a ball of flames.

The plane's nose tore through the security fence like it was made of gauze, sparks spraying as the twisted metal lodged underneath dragged along the concrete. Now it was time to pray. Which saint should I address my message to? St. Patrick's Day was tomorrow, but he wasn't a fellow I thought much about outside of his special day. He was the big one, the patron saint of Ireland. His inbox would be full. I liked to check in with the littler guys who maybe didn't receive as many prayers. Maybe they weren't as powerful in a spiritual sense, but at least you knew they would put their all into your request. There were a couple of patron saints of aviation, but they were fairly obscure to a layman like myself. I'd have to look them up on my phone, which was time I didn't have.

"Holy Mary, Mother of God!" I yelled.

And, just like that, the plane skidded to a stop amidst the trees, yards from plowing onto the interstate. Ah, Mary. Worked every time.

Onboard, everything had gone quiet. The lights flickered off again, causing a collective gasp. This was followed by a collective exhale as the lights came back on. Backup power. The flight attendant, still strapped in, had a growing wet spot on the front of his navy pants. His hair seemed to be standing taller than before.

Through the rain-spattered windows, there were flashes of yellow and red. Emergency vehicles on the way.

A sharp *THWACK* at my window sent my heart a-fluttering. It wasn't a leprechaun or gremlin — it was a tree branch that had snapped. The wind was dragging it back and forth across the window. I shuddered at the brush with mortality, at the absurdity of the whole damned situation. Then the shuddering turned into chuckling.

Good thing I was alone in first class.

By the time I'd regained my composure, the first responders were boarding. The poor flight attendant strapped in like a baby in his carrier still hadn't moved. He was babbling to the medics about Joe Biden and the Virgin Mary. He was the only one wheeled off on a stretcher, far as I know.

While the firefighters were helping the rest of us deplane one by one, I learned that the pilot had attempted to stop while on the runway. She was under the mistaken impression there was some sort of medical emergency on board involving Joe Biden. (The attendant's handset had cut in and out.) The brakes locked up due to the slick runway, and that's when things had gone to H. E. double toothpicks in a handbasket.

Before I stepped off the plane, I shook the pilot's hand. She had long blond hair and reminded me of Jill. "No medical emergency here," I explained. "I may be seventy-six, but this baby's still in mint condition."

I caught a ride back to the terminal in a covered golf cart.

I never did get that bag of peanuts.

41

I trudged through the puddles on the downtown sidewalks in my worn-down loafers. With every step, I could feel the wet muck squish between my toes. I didn't want to think about what was in it. The rain was cleaning the pavement of the day's festivities, washing the filth into the storm drains and, eventually, the Chicago River.

Across the street from the Tribune Tower, I stopped for the crosswalk.

There was no cross-traffic. I could have stepped into the street, but I was frozen in place, staring up at the imposing gothic building from beneath my umbrella. Barack was up there, on the twenty-fifth floor foyer. So, presumably, was a stone-cold criminal who'd suckered the president and everyone else in Barack's orbit.

Neither Steve nor Michelle had answered my calls, which meant I'd be walking into the situation blind. I had no plan other than to make a scene. I'd already made a horse's ass of myself in front of Barack once today. What did I have to lose?

Lightning flashed and a thunderclap shattered the calm. The streets and sidewalks were all but deserted. Everyone who would normally have been hitting the bars on a Saturday night was at home, hungover from the parade. The rain was a cold one. Every drop that hit my cheeks stung like a slap in the face. The cheap umbrella I'd picked up from the Jewel-Osco down the street wasn't holding up in the wind, so I stuffed it in the trash. The good news was that the rain might have put a damper on the crime wave predicted for the weekend. That, and I'd grabbed some honey-roasted nuts at the drugstore.

A figure in a khaki trench coat stopped next to me. The DON'T WALK signal was still lit, but I held my ground. No sense jumping the gun. Almost time to storm the castle. Any moment now and I'd step into the crosswalk, and the countdown would be on. It was game time — go big or go home. Barack had taught me that. When he'd failed to win a state senate seat, he hadn't headed home from Springfield with his tail between his legs. He'd set his sights on the U.S. Senate instead. Go big or go home.

I planned to go big *and* go home. I'd already texted Jill to let her know that my plane had run into mechanical trouble, and that I was trying to reschedule for another flight. It was mostly true.

The crosswalk sign changed. I held back a moment to let the other pedestrian go ahead of me. When they didn't move, I took a longer look. The wide body, the André the Giant hands, the rain pitter-pattering off his shaved scalp. Benny "Bento Box" Polaski. Rahm's right-hand man didn't have an umbrella. He'd probably never used an umbrella in his life, the deviant.

I had to remain calm. I couldn't show weakness. If only I hadn't been munching those peanuts. My mouth was dry, and I desperately needed a glass of water. As it was, I couldn't do much beyond swallow as hard as I could to try to work up some saliva so I could say something, anything.

"Hello, Joe," Bento Box said, a hard candy clacking against his teeth. There was another flash of lightning, followed not by thunder but by the fixer's low, rumbling laughter.

42

I tensed up, preparing to shield myself in case Bento Box came at me with a right or left hook. Protect my face, protect my chest. Try not to pass out from the pain. And then fight back. Fight back until I couldn't swing my arms no more. *Dinner is for winners, Joey. Dinner is for winners.*

"Heard your plane ran into some trouble," he said.

"Nobody was hurt."

"That's very fortunate. You're a lucky man."

Luck had nothing to do with it. The pilots knew their stuff and were the ones who should have been praised for avoiding certain disaster.

The crosswalk signal was flashing now. A police car passed us in the other direction without slowing.

"You need to ask yourself," I told Bento Box, "whether this is worth it."

He cocked his head, examining me curiously.

"Ask yourself if *he's* worth it," I said.

"The president?"

"Your boss," I said. "Do what you want to me, but ask yourself if he's worth it. Is this really what you want to be doing? Trying to beat up a septuagenarian?"

"You think I'm going to beat you up?"

"You're going to try. I didn't say you were going to be successful."

The signal stopped flashing.

A pair of headlights was headed toward the intersection. It wasn't time to walk; it was time to run. I dashed into the street, right in the path of the oncoming vehicle, confident that the fixer wouldn't follow.

"Wait! Joe!" Bento Box shouted.

The headlights blinded me. It didn't look like the driver was slowing down. I pushed myself into second gear and reached the opposite curb as the car's brakes squealed.

There was a *THUMP* behind me. I glanced over my shoulder and saw Bento Box lying on his back on the hood of the stopped sedan. The front of the car was crumpled, as if it'd hit a concrete pole. A four-foot-wide concrete pole.

The car backed up quickly, and Bento Box rolled off onto the pavement. Then it spun around the fixer's body and ran through the light as it turned red. By the time the shock wore off, the car was already several blocks away. I hadn't thought to write down the plate.

The rain was letting up. After looking both ways, I ran to the lump in the street.

Bento Box was on his back. There was a dark pool growing under his head. The Werther's he'd been sucking was all the way in the other lane.

I tried to get him to his feet, but he was down and out. I called 911 to report the accident and then, using my lower back muscles, dragged him unceremoniously to the curb, where I sat him against a sign like a sack of trash. The front of my shirt was stained with his blood. The cut on his scalp was wide, but not deep. It continued to gush. I wrapped my jacket around my forearm and applied pressure to the wound.

Without warning, the fixer's eyes popped open. He reached out for me with one giant mitt. I thought he was about to strangle me, but he latched onto my shirt collar instead of my throat. He pulled me close. "Listen, I came to tell you . . . it's Caruso . . ."

"The rapper."

"He's pulling all the strings . . . the Crooks . . . the police . . . everyone. This

266

whole town is corrupt. I took his money. We all did."

His voice was weak and raspy. Compensating for crushed ribs. Bento Box had a lot of padding. It was the only reason he was still breathing.

"Why are you telling me this?" I asked.

He grinned. His teeth were stained red. "If I'm going to die, I can't die . . . a bad guy."

"You're not going to die," I said, holding his hand as sirens wailed in the distance. I looked away, unable to meet his eyes for fear that he'd know I was lying.

43

There was no visible security on display outside the Tribune Tower. Van Heusen and the horse-mounted cops must have been sent home for the day after the protestors and parade-goers had cleared out. I'd still need to get past building security at the front desk, and possibly one or two Secret Service agents. Barack's detail would recognize me. It was far from a given they would let me upstairs. Had Steve ordered them to hold me, to keep me from causing a scene?

I had to find another way to the Crown foyer.

Since hang-gliding onto the roof from a neighboring building was out of the question — Barack was the hang-glider, not me — I decided to go underground. Specifically, through the parking garage below the building. I hustled past the unmanned card-reading tollbooth at the street-level exit, keeping my head down. Benny "Bento Box"

Polaski was being tended to by medics, but I didn't have time to concern myself with him. What I was looking for was a tenant's-only entrance to the tower. The *Tribune* employees didn't use the revolving doors out front. Whatever doors I found down here would require a badge, but if I could time it right —

There. A glass door with a magnetized card reader. A man in an overcoat stepping out. I hustled through the parked cars, past the man. He wasn't paying me any attention. He was going through his pockets, probably looking for his keys. I stuck a hand inside the door, inches from closing. It was heavy, and it bit down on my fingers. I stifled a yelp.

"Hey," the guy said.

I took a deep breath and turned. My heart was pounding.

"You got a light?" he asked, holding up a cigarette between two fingers.

I pretended to pat down my pockets. Wouldn't you know, it wasn't just for show — I still had the lighter I'd snatched from the record store fella. Mr. Ponytail.

"Keep it," I said, tossing it to the smoker.

"You're a lifesaver."

Time would tell. Time would tell . . .

There wasn't any security at the elevator

bank inside the tenant's-only entrance. There was, unfortunately, a magnetic key-card pad on every one of the five elevators. The only way up would be to hitch a ride with somebody. That wasn't happening. My dress shirt was stained as red as the stripes on the flag. It was only through the grace of God that the man looking for a light hadn't seen me from the front as I'd run past.

I poked my head into the emergency stairwell, since it didn't require a magnetic card for access. The stairs went round and round and would take me all the way to the twenty-fifth floor. I pulled off my shoes, emptied the water that had soaked through, and fit them back on.

I'd been training in cities around the country for this very moment. I was the Stair Master.

44

Three flights up, and I was huffing and puffing like the Big Bad Wolf up against the pig in the brick house. You would have thought it was my first day on a treadmill in a quarter century. I'd been hitting the gym plenty, sometimes twice a day. Unfortunately, real stairs were a lot more difficult than a StairMaster. For one thing, I couldn't control the resistance. For another, I couldn't take a ten-minute break to wipe my brow, refill my water bottle, and check Politico.

I didn't even have a water bottle.

All I could do was push on, taking each step like it was my first . . . or last.

My heart was pounding, trying to break out of my ribs like a caged wombat. Sweat had erupted from every pore — under my arms, on my forehead. Everywhere but my rump (poor Steve).

The cramp in my side started around the

tenth floor, stabbing me in the gut like a butcher knife. Two floors later, the cramping hit my calves, locking them up tight. My knees were rusty hinges that didn't work right on the best of days; I'd be lucky not to tear an ACL again, like I had a few summers ago. I took three more steps, each one like sinking into quicksand. My legs were weights now, burdens that I was dragging up the staircase like the thin, wobbly, unwieldy things they were. *If only I'd trained harder, if only I hadn't taken so many breaks, if only, if only, if only . . .*

I sat down on the twelfth-floor platform. *Catching my breath,* I told myself. *Just a breather.*

The cool metal of the railing dug into my back. The stairwell was unheated. That, combined with the fact that my clothes were soaking wet and bloody to boot, meant that I was colder than a well-digger's behind.

I peeled off my shoes and tried once again to empty the water. It was useless. Same with my socks, which refused any effort to wring them dry. I hurled one shoe against the wall in frustration. It ricocheted at an angle, and disappeared over the railing.

It landed at the bottom of the staircase with an echoing slap.

Thirteen more floors. Almost halfway

there. I could see the stairwell ceiling, hundreds of feet above. Below me, the view was equally dizzying. I still had my phone — I could try Steve again. I already knew that was useless, though. I could try building security and ask them to get ahold of the Secret Service upstairs. Would they believe me? A former vice president who'd lost a shoe?

My breathing was returning to normal, but I was losing precious time. My muscles were still tensed up. As soon as I tried to mount the stairs again, the cramp in my side would return. I'd been a runner long enough to know that once that happened, you were screwed for the rest of the day. Better off trying again tomorrow, and the next day, and the next day, until your body got used to the workout.

I didn't have days.

If I was doing this for myself, I wouldn't have gotten back on my bare feet. But I wasn't doing it for myself. I was doing it for Barack, to warn him his friend was dangerous, a suspicion now confirmed by Rahm's fixer. I was doing it for everyone who'd been screwed by a corrupt system, for everyone who couldn't fight back.

I was doing it for Shaun.

I got up and cracked my neck. I left my

socks and other penny loafer behind. I took the stairs one by one, without looking up, oblivious to the pain and the useless muscles, like a marathon runner in the last five-mile stretch, past the point of sweating, pushing myself through the stars firing at the edges of my vision, all the way to the twenty-fifth floor, where I collapsed through the stairwell door and into the reception room in a messy, bloody heap as my vision went black.

45

When I came to, Michelle Obama was kneeling over me. I was on my back in so much pain that I couldn't pinpoint one place that hurt on my body. It *all* hurt. Michelle had a concerned look on her face. Then again, that was a look she had a lot of the time when I was around.

"Barack," I said. I had exerted every bit of energy and then some climbing the stairs, and now I sounded exactly like the frail old man my critics charged me with being. "Where's . . . Barack . . ."

An aide held a plastic cup to my lips. I drank thirstily until water spilled out and ran down my chin.

"Can you sit up?" Michelle asked. "That might help."

I propped myself up. For the first time, I noticed that my button-down shirt had been unbuttoned — someone must have mistaken the blood for my own. There was no time to explain.

"Where is he?" I asked.

Michelle handed me the cup but didn't answer my question. "Don't take this the wrong way, Joe, but you look like a drowned rat."

I chugged the rest of the water in one massive gulp. "Meanwhile, you look stunning as ever. I'm not just blowing smoke, either."

She sent her aide off to refill the cup. I appreciated Michelle's kindness — her motherly instinct, you might say. But I didn't have the time to thank her.

"I'll send someone to get you a change of clothes," she said, looking me up and down.

I started buttoning my shirt. "Is this a black-tie event?"

"You're going to need more than a tie, Joe. Whose blood is this?"

"The Kool-Aid Man's."

"I raised two kids. I know the difference between Kool-Aid and blood."

I coughed. "There was an accident out front."

Her eyes grew wide.

"Nobody you know, don't worry."

"Is everyone OK? Barack told me what happened to Shaun this morning. I saw a few missed calls from you . . ."

276

"This was a hit and run," I said. "I helped the victim up and he's on the way to the hospital. That's what happened to my shirt — no good deed goes unpunished."

"I'll say. You gave him your shoes?"

I looked at my pink toes. "He was barefoot. Anyone else would have done the same. If they wore the same size."

"Bono better watch out — there's a new Good Samaritan in town."

"Heh," I said. I wasn't sure who Bono was. It was the sort of name you'd give a circus monkey. "I was on my way to crash the reception."

"You're on the wrong floor, then." The doors opened onto a veranda. The Crown foyer. There was no one outside. "We all went down to the lower-level ballroom when it started raining. Took forever to move everyone in the elevators. I assume that's why you took the stairs?"

All that work . . . for nothing. Story of my life.

Michelle explained that the Secret Service found me here while clearing the last of the guests. They had called her upstairs to check on me since they couldn't reach Barack.

"He's not here?" I asked, visions of kidnapping flashing through my mind. My wrists still chafed from the rope earlier in the evening.

"Barack went out boating with Caruso."
She rolled her eyes. "You know how it is.
Boys and their toys."

46

Barack Obama was in trouble. How much remained to be seen. I gave Michelle some babble about the rain and wind, how I wouldn't have gone out on a boat in weather like this. My flight had been canceled, after all. Just to be on the safe side, she had one of her Service agents call Steve, who had accompanied Barack onto Lake Michigan.

"No answer," the agent reported back. "The storm must be interfering with the cell tower servicing the lake. The weather is almost past. I'm sure Steve checked out the lake conditions before they went out — he would have stopped Renegade if it was unsafe."

While Steve got on my last nerve at times, he was a capable agent, as he'd demonstrated time and again. He could be tough on us, but it was for our own safety. He reminded me of my old babysitter in Scranton, and how she'd let us Bidens have an extra scoop of ice cream — but only if we cleared the veggies off our plates.

Michelle, satisfied that her husband wasn't in imminent danger, turned to me. "You need someplace to stay tonight?"

"I'm a little too old to crash on the couch."

"We have a guest room, you know."

"I assumed *Le Château de Obamas* would be booked solid, what with the Secret Service, and the house sitter, and the cook, and the yoga instructor, and . . ."

She led me to the elevator. Some of my strength had returned. "The agents stay in hotels, unless they're on duty. Where do yours stay?"

I looked away.

She slapped her forehead. "Of course. I'm sorry. I forgot you only got that six-month detail and then . . ."

"I appreciate the offer, Michelle. I'll have to see if my travel agent has booked me a hotel first. Then I might grab a little late-night snack and see what kind of trouble I can get into before swinging by."

The elevator opened. Her aide stepped out with a black garment bag. Inside was a pair of dress shoes and one of President Obama's skinny-cut navy suits. It was a shade darker than mine, and cost more than my monthly mortgages and car leases combined.

Michelle measured it against me. "I had my staff pick this up so that he could change out of that hideous tan get-up. But he's not here, and you are. You can change in the men's room down the hall. Feel free to come downstairs and grab a bite to eat in the ballroom if you want — the party's going to keep going as long as we can afford the DJ."

"What's a DJ cost, a hundred bucks an hour?"

"This is Questlove. He doesn't get out of bed for under ten grand."

"Must be nice," I said. I took the garment bag from Michelle. The suit would fit — Barack and I were close in height and weight, even though he had more lean muscle mass.

"Oh, and Joe," she said on her way out. "Next time, take the elevator."

And with that, I was alone again.

I washed up in the men's room before changing. Paper towels and a sink. What we used to call a "hobo bath." I busied my mind with ways to get to Caruso's yacht. Would I charter a helicopter? Rent a boat? Could you do either one of those this late on a Saturday night? I hadn't wanted to alarm Michelle that her husband was in trouble because doubt had started to creep into my mind. What if Caruso simply wanted to take an evening boat ride? The more I thought about it, the more I realized he had no way to know I was on to him. He didn't know that Bento Box had given him up to me. There was no need to panic.

The button-down shirtsleeves on Barack's dress shirt were about an inch too long — and I couldn't button the jacket around my midsection — but Barack's suit fit better than expected. I didn't look half bad when I did a pose-off in front of the full-length mirror next to the hand dryers.

I slipped on my Ray-Bans and made two finger-guns in the mirror. So this is what a million bucks felt like. Not bad. Not bad at all.

I mustered up a semi-serious frown and addressed the man in the mirror: "There's not a liberal America and a conservative America; there's the United States of America." I imagined the cheering throngs of voters, clamoring for hope and change. "There's not a Black America and White America and Latino America and Asian America; there's the United States of America."

I smiled from cheek to cheek and waved,

thanking the imaginary crowd for their support. "Thank you very much, everybody. God bless you. Thank you. Thank you."

It was so real, I could hear the clapping. It took me longer than it should have to realize the clapping wasn't in my head . . . it was coming from the doorway, where Barack Obama was leaning against the tiled wall, clapping slowly and thunderously, a plodding beat that grew ever louder, echoing through the restroom like a drumbeat for the damned.

47

I busied myself by stuffing my bloody clothes into the trash. How long had he been standing there? I was glad Barack was alive and well, but I had ostrich egg on my face and he knew it.

Scratch that — he was *enjoying* it.

"What happened to your excursion on the lake?" I asked.

"Same thing that happened to your flight. There was a little . . . delay."

"A delay? You guys are still going? It's getting late, isn't it?"

"I know why you're here, Joe."

"I'm here to do a little schmoozing. Can't let Oprah bag all the big donors."

He frowned at me. "You're worried about her running for president. As a Democrat. Sorry to break this to you, but she was here to see Michelle. I think they were discussing doing more events together when *Becoming* is out in paperback. And, just so you know, the reception downstairs is packed with economics professors and grad students. Not exactly big-time donors."

I soaped up my hands. "So she's not running."

"What do you think?"

"I believed her when she told the media she wasn't. Now . . ."

"You should believe her, Joe. She's easy to see through when she's not being honest. Kind of reminds me of somebody else I know."

I couldn't meet his eyes.

"This isn't about her or what happens in the next two years," Barack said.

"No, it's not. You're right." I finally looked at him. "It's about your friend."

"Caruso," he said. "He and I left the reception early. He told me he wanted to talk about Shaun. Had something to show me. That's when he got a call on his phone. Same Blackberry model as mine. I realized what I should have seen earlier if only I hadn't been so blind: Caruso was the one who'd picked up my phone. By accident."

"What happened next was no accident," I said.

"Wish I could say you were wrong."

"So he was at the freight yard. Did he pull the trigger?"

"Did Charles Manson kill anyone with his own hands?" Barack said. "Did Bin Laden?"

"Have you talked to the police?"

He shook his head. "Caruso has deep pockets. You can buy anything in Chicago, including, as we've seen, protection."

"It's a good thing you didn't report him," I said. I told him about my run-in with Bento Box. We were between a rock and a hard place (probably another rock, let's be honest). "Did Caruso head back to his penthouse apartment high atop the city?"

"He's not a super-villain, Joe. He lives in the suburbs." Barack snorted. "Naperville. Although he's —"

I aired my hands out under the dryer, which was loud enough to drown out the rest of what Barack was saying.

"Sorry," I shouted. "This damn thing —"

He raised his voice: "I said he's on the lake. When I bowed out, he said he was going out alone. Only I don't think he's alone. I think he has Shaun."

The air dryer went silent.

"There was supposed to be security," I said.

"Frisking for weapons. Stopping someone from trying to finish the job. But not stopping Shaun from leaving."

"Shaun left on his own?"

Barack shook his head. "He was still sedated. Not alert. Somebody took him for a ride in a stolen wheelchair, straight out a service entrance. Security cameras had been cut, so we think whoever did this had inside help. The receptionist remembers seeing a 'big man' on the floor. Sound like anyone you know?"

Caruso was six and a half feet tall. If he'd orchestrated the initial hit this morning, it made sense for him to spring Shaun so he could tie up the loose end. We were still missing a motive. It had something to do with that stolen shipment of firearms. The blanks would fill themselves in once we showed him the jig was up.

"What makes you think he has Shaun on his boat?" I said.

"The stolen wheelchair is pinging GPS on Lake Michigan."

"They can track wheelchairs now?"

"Wheelchairs aren't cheap, Joe. Makes sense to do some inventory control."

"Damn." I shook my head. "You know Caruso best. You think he's capable of something like this?"

"If you go by the lyrics on his early albums, he's capable of this and a whole lot more. Rap isn't real life, though. He was in a gang, sure. He dealt heroin. Did he ever kill anyone? He says he came close, and that was a turning point in his life. He's all about being a positive role model now. His record sales took a nosedive, but he's a changed man. He's bigger than his music. He's been talking about running for mayor. But now . . ."

"If somebody can change for the better," I said, "what's to say they can't also change for the worse?"

"I'll believe it when I see it," Barack said. "Straighten your tie."

Mobilizing a Secret Service assault team wasn't an option. This wasn't their fight. Plus, we both knew we had to play the situation delicately. If there was any chance that Shaun was still alive on that boat, we couldn't show up in force. As soon as Caruso heard sirens, he would know it was the endgame. We needed to take him by surprise or not take him at all. The last thing he would expect would be for President Obama and Vice President Biden to come knocking on his door, alone and unarmed.

48

Barack found us a boat nearby, docked on the riverbank. It was a massive single-story vessel used for river and lake tours during the day. It was also a wreck. The boat was older than Methuselah, judging by the rusted metal and rotted wood holding it together. But it would have to do.

The tour boat captain was a Cuban American woman wearing a T-shirt that read I'VE GOT CRABS. We'd met up with her across the street from the Tribune Tower in an underground tavern, which was at the bottom of a grimy staircase. Over cheeseburgers, Barack and the woman — Gonzalez — had hashed out details of their plan. At one point, the captain nodded in my direction and asked, in a hushed tone, "He cool?"

"Am I cool?" I'd said. I couldn't help raising my voice. "I'm so cool they call me Joe Cool."

"They call Snoopy 'Joe Cool,' " Gonzalez said.

"Where do you think Chuck Schulz got the name?"

As Gonzalez was untying the boat from the dock, Barack and I sat down on one of the dozen onboard metal bleachers meant for tourists.

"You didn't back me up there at the tavern," I whispered.

"Back you up?"

I shifted on the cold metal. "The Joe Cool thing."

"I've never heard anyone call you that. That's the truth. Now, I've heard other names: Amtrak Joe, the Uncle-in-Chief . . ."

"The Uncle-in-Chief?"

"Don't think too hard about it."

That was easy for Barack Obama to say. Try as he might to earn my sympathy for his "plight" as "the cool president," he was the coolest guy I knew. He was the coolest guy *anyone* knew.

"This is beginning to seem like a bad idea," Steve said, standing alert next to the president. He looked like he was ready to throw up.

"It didn't seem like one before?" Barack said.

"No, it definitely did. How sure are you

guys that this is the right thing to do? My job is on the line. If something happens . . ."

Barack shrugged. "There's a chance we're wrong. There's a chance we're right."

"How sure are you that you're right?"

"You want a number? I'd say . . . seventy percent. With a three percent margin of error."

Steve snorted. "You've had your pollsters working on this."

"I let all my pollsters go," Barack said. The engine started and the air filled with the sweet smell of burning gasoline.

"Enough numbers," I said. I'd been advocating for Barack to trust his instincts for years. All that badgering seemed to have finally taken root. "Have you seen what's happened to baseball? You have to be a statistician to understand half these new stats. OPS? What in halitosis does that even mean?"

"On-base Plus Slugging," Barack said.

I rolled my eyes. "Like I said, I have no idea what any of that means. I was a solid C student. I did what I had to do to get by. Sometimes, you have to throw everything you know out the window and trust your gut."

We had no real plan of which to speak. All I knew was that it was time to put up or shut up.

The Bidens had never bowed down to bullies. Never. Ma Biden raised us to give as good as we got. Trouble was, the world had changed since I was a kid. Disagreements weren't settled by fisticuffs in the Senate. You couldn't even joke about taking someone out under the bleachers and teaching them a lesson without folks getting their tighty-whities in a bunch.

But Barack and I weren't in Washington right now. We were in Chicago. The rules of engagement were different. It was time to go punch the bully in the mouth.

That's Chicago, baby.

49

We cut through the harbor lock into Lake Michigan, joining dozens of boats on the open water. Gonzalez had already pinpointed Caruso a half mile offshore. His boat wasn't hard to miss. It was the hundred-and-thirty-foot black luxury yacht with the red pinstripe.

The rain had died down. The storm, however, continued, as lightning flashed across the sky in brilliant arcs. Every muscle in my legs ached, and would for a while. What I needed was a nice, long, warm bath. Candles weren't necessary, but I wouldn't say no to a lavender bath bomb.

Barack emerged from the cabin and unlocked a storage floorboard. "Looks like some trouble ahead. Joe, you and I are going below deck until the coast is clear." He turned to Steve. "Gonzalez wants to speak with you."

I craned my neck to see into the murky

pit. "Below deck? Through that hole?"

"Not through the hole," Barack said. "In the hole."

Two human beings in there — let alone one — seemed an impossibility, like packing a king-size comforter and bedding set into a single washer.

Barack read the skeptical look on my face. "Gonzalez once had six guys down there. Big guys, too — well fed."

All I could think was, *Why?*

Steve looked unsure about it all, but he kept his mouth shut as he closed the hatch on me and Barack.

Everything went dark as the depths of the lake. Barack and I huddled together, arms and legs twisted like a couple of pretzels. We'd been in close quarters before and survived.

"What kind of trouble was the captain talking about?" I asked in a whisper.

"There's a small boat headed our way. Probably nothing, but it could be the police."

"We're not doing anything illegal."

"You remember what your friend Polaski said."

We sat in darkness for a beat. All you could hear was the sound of us breathing, and the splash of the surf on the underside of the boat.

"Listen, Joe, there's something we need to talk about."

"About what happened with the pastor . . . I'm sorry. I —"

"Hold up a sec," he said. "What I have to say is important, and I want you to listen. I was going to tell you this earlier, at the speakeasy, but we were interrupted. Just wait until I'm finished before you say anything. Got it?"

"Go ahead."

"We've been through a lot together, you and I. Two long, grueling campaigns for the White House. Two terms in office, fighting Congress every step of the way. It was always going to be an uphill climb, but I didn't know the Senate and House would be rolling boulders down that hill, trying to knock us back."

I could have told him that was going to happen, but would he have listened? Experience is the best teacher. Painful, but effective.

"We didn't get off on the right foot," he continued. "We didn't always see eye to eye. But we were always honest with each other. Remember what you said — that if something big ever came between us that we couldn't hash out, if you had some moral objection to the road we were going down, you would let me know."

"And I'd resign," I said. "We'd tell the press I had prostate cancer. So that you could save face."

"Would you have done it?"

At the time I'd proposed the scheme, I'd been dead certain I could do it — as a thought exercise, it didn't require any effort. The public had a right to know what was happening behind closed doors in Washington, but their right to know had limits. Especially when it came to family. And Barack Obama was nothing if not family.

"I'd have done something," I said, finally. "I'd have come up with some story. I wouldn't have left you swinging your wedding tackle in the wind."

"Is that a Delaware saying?"

"It's something Ted Kennedy used to say."

"Fascinating. What I'm getting at here, Joe, is that we don't keep stuff from each other — even if we know we're going to upset the other person. Even if what we're going to say may offend the other person, and even if it's going to come between us. Do you see what I'm getting at?"

I swallowed hard. "I think so."

"What I'm trying to say is, don't take this

the wrong way . . . but if you let out one more of them old man Bloomin' Onion seam-splitters in here, I'm going to feed you to the catfish."

I clenched my butt cheeks tight as a snare drum. I hadn't even been aware that my air whistle was letting off steam. "It's not me," I said. "You've got the wrong man."

"Joe."

"I'm being serious," I said.

"Yeah? Then tell me: where'd you eat last night?"

Outback Steakhouse.

He had me dead to rights, and he knew it. Son of a gumshoe.

"You're mad," he said.

"I'm not."

"I don't understand why you get mad about this stuff, Joe. Everybody farts."

"*Everybody Farts.* Is that one of the books you're writing on your new contract?"

"I wrote one picture book. That was enough —"

A voice amplified by a megaphone interrupted us, and we both went quiet. We couldn't make out what was being said, but it sounded authoritative. Gonzalez barked something back, and then more megaphone. This went back and forth for a few minutes while we held our breath.

Footsteps overhead. We'd been boarded.

There were hushed voices, and then somebody shouted. More shouting. Things were getting heated. Maybe I could de-escalate the situation. I'd helped bridge the partisan divide in the Senate on many occasions. Plus, I had to cut one something fierce and didn't want to do so in close quarters with Barack.

"I'm going up," I whispered, untangling my body from his.

"Don't be stupid."

"Your friend is putting her life on the line for us. If there's trouble, we need to take care of it before it gets out of hand."

"She's somebody who owes me a favor. Not a friend, but she's discreet and comes highly recommended. I'm sure she can talk her way out of it. She's a tour guide, after all."

"I thought she was a captain?"

"She's the captain of a tour boat, Joe. That makes her a tour guide."

"Well, I'm going to do her a favor, and then she'll owe me," I said, pushing up the floorboard. "Cover me."

"Cover you?" Barack shouted after me, but it was too late. I was out. We'd been under deck for five minutes. It was long enough that I'd almost forgotten what the outside world looked like. I hadn't been down there so long, however, that I'd forgotten what staring down the barrel of a gun looked like.

A pale twentysomething was pointing a semi-automatic AR-style rifle in my face. He smiled, showing off two rows of gold teeth. A speedboat was docked off to the side, and the two boats were roped together. The speedboat was flying a black flag with a silver skull and crossbones. The same stylized symbol tattooed on Caruso. Only now I could see the crossbones weren't bones at all. They were handguns.

50

The first time I had a gun pointed at me was when I'd made a trip to Afghanistan with a couple of fellow senators a decade and a half ago. Our helicopter had gone down in hostile territory, leading to a tense encounter between our group of American politicians and Taliban-aligned forces. The full details had never made the news rounds, but suffice to say we'd all made it out alive thanks to some fast-acting Marines.

There wouldn't be any Marines to save us now.

"Come on out of there," the man with the gold teeth said. "Hands in the air. Don't try anything funny."

I did as instructed, letting the floorboard fall behind me.

It landed on Goldie's foot.

"Hold on," he said, kicking it back up. "Your friend, too."

Barack crawled out of the hold and joined

me. The city, lit up green for the holiday, glittered in the distance. The other yachts and tour boats on the lake were too far away to hear our screams. Too far to hear gunshots.

Goldie wasn't alone. He had a friend with hoop earrings and an eyepatch. The friend was armed with two semi-automatic rifles, as if he could even fire both at the same time without accidentally shooting up half the Midwest.

Gonzalez was slumped over against one of the posts supporting the boat's upper deck. Blood trickled from one of her ears.

I didn't see Steve.

"Mr. Obama," Goldie said. "Welcome home."

"I believe you have mistaken me for someone else," Barack said.

Goldie got right up in Barack's face. He tugged on one of his ears. "No, I believe it is you. *El presidente de los Estados Unidos.*"

Barack didn't flinch.

"And you must be his friend," Goldie said, motioning toward me with the barrel of his gun. "The Uncle-in-Chief."

"I'll tell you who I am," I said. "I'm Joe Biden. And I want to be the first to welcome you to our vessel. We have no quarrel with lake pirates —"

"Pirates?" One-Eyed Willie said. "You think because I have an eyepatch that we're *pirates*? Do you see Johnny Depp anywhere around here?"

"We don't have any money on us," Barack said.

"I have a few bucks," I said, patting my wallet.

Barack stared holes into me.

"You think this is about money?" Goldie said.

"We don't have drugs, either," I said. "Some vitamins in a pillbox that my wife gave me for my birthday last year. I have low Vitamin D levels, and I need the calcium to ward off osteoporosis —"

"There's the two of you?" he asked. "No more?"

I glanced around. Steve was still MIA. Had they already done away with him?

"You're free to inspect the boat," I said. Gonzalez didn't interrupt, as she was unconscious. "We chartered this boat —"

"We know where you're going," One-Eyed Willie said. "And we're here to escort you."

"That's very kind of you."

He laughed. "You're a little late for the party, guys, but there's plenty of room . . . at the bottom of the lake." He motioned his gun toward us. "Turn around."

His friend patted us down. They weren't pirates, of course. They were Crooks. They didn't have any intention of taking us back to their boss's yacht. Not if they could take care of us here. The one with the eyepatch hadn't meant that crack about the bottom of the lake as a joke.

There was no way they would use their weapons on us, though. They meant to drown us and sink our boat. Make it look like an accident. If we washed up onshore riddled with bullets, the crackdown on crime around town would be so swift and severe that Caruso's operations would be crippled.

I dropped my hands.

"Did I say you could put your hands down?" Goldie said.

"This isn't Simon Says." I could see Barack out of the side of my eye, his arms still up. His eyes were wide as saucers.

Goldie patted his rifle. "This is Simon. And Simon says, 'Put your hands in the air before I punch holes in that fancy suit of yours.'"

I should have been afraid, but a calm had come over me. The guns were just for show, to scare us into getting in the water.

"I'm giving you to the count of three to drop your weapons and get on your knees, hands behind your head," I said, holding my ground.

One-Eyed Willie laughed. "And if we don't?"

I cracked my knuckles. "I'm going to beat you like a couple of government mules."

"Joe," Barack hissed.

"One," I said. My eyes were fixed on the shocked Crooks, who were exchanging worried looks. *The old man is crazy! What do we do?*

"Two."

They raised all three rifles at me. I stood my ground, but doubt had crept into my mind. Maybe they were trying to call my bluff. What if their boss wasn't a micromanager? What if he'd left the decision of how best to deal with us up to them?

"Two and a half," I said. My pulse was up now. My feet were quaking in Barack's shoes. They were a size too big, so there was plenty of room to quake in them.

Before I could get to two and three-quarters, the Crook with the golden teeth dropped to his knees. The gun slipped from his hands. He faceplanted right on top of it, skull and metal colliding with a sickening *THUMP.* One-Eyed Willie watched his friend fall, and then he toppled, unconscious, into a pile of guns and flesh.

Steve was standing tall behind the downed men, dripping wet like he'd just crawled out of Lake Michigan. In fact, he *had* just crawled out of Lake Michigan. He was breathing heavy.

"Steve! How long were you in the water?" I asked.

"A few seconds. I swam around from the back of the boat."

"You learn to swim like that when you were in the well?"

Steve ignored my question. "Are you OK, Mr. President?"

"Fine," Barack said.

"Me too," I added. "I'm also fine."

Steve used some rope he found lying around to tie the Crooks to a railing, winding it around their torsos.

"What kind of knot are you using there?" I asked. I knew a few different seaman's knots. My uncle, who claimed to be the basis for the old man in *The Old Man and the Sea,* had taught me the art of knot tying one summer. It wasn't until years later that I read the novel and discovered that my uncle — in his late thirties that summer, an ancient man to me at the time — wasn't nearly old enough to be the protagonist of Hemingway's book.

"What kind of knot?" Steve said. "One

that will hold them."

Barack helped Gonzalez into a sitting position. The captain was awake, but woozy. She confessed, through slurred speech, that she'd sold us out. She was damned sorry for it, but she had family to think of, and didn't we know who we were up against?

"We're beginning to get an idea," I said. Gonzalez's head tipped forward. When I leaned her back, her eyes were slack.

"We need to get her to a hospital," I said. I held up my phone, trying to get bars. Nothing.

"My phone's at the bottom of the lake," Steve said, climbing down the ladder. "I checked the radio. They smashed it. We might have to wait until the cell towers are working again and try yours, Joe, or —"

Barack fished the tour boat's keys out of Gonzalez's pocket. He tossed them to Steve. "Head for the city lights. You can't miss it."

"You guys untie the speedboat," Steve said. "Let it loose. I'll pull up anchor."

I hated to see a good speedboat go to waste, but we hadn't found the keys in either of the Crooks' pockets. It was deadweight to us.

Steve returned to the cabin. The water around us bubbled as the engine started. Caruso's yacht sat in the distance like a floating fortress. It was a good quarter-mile away, anchored in place. Waiting for the speedboat to return.

"What's going to happen to Shaun?" I said.

Barack pulled the speedboat close. "I want to believe Caruso will come to his senses. Maybe the Crooks have something on him, and they're forcing him to do this."

I worked on one of the knots. It was tighter than Grandma Biden's girdle. "Believe what you want, but Shaun is in danger either way."

He followed my eyes to the luxury yacht. "We need to get Gonzalez medical attention ASAP. They cracked her on the skull — she could have bleeding in her brain. Without relieving the pressure, she's as good as dead. We can either keep on course or we can return to shore. We already lost the element of surprise, so my vote is on the latter."

"Gonzalez betrayed us."

"That doesn't make her life worth any less. She may have betrayed us, but she's still a human being."

I knew it. I didn't like it, but I knew it. We weren't in a position to judge. Perhaps no man is, when it comes to the life of another. That's God's domain, not ours.

One rope was all that tethered the speed-boat to ours. Suddenly, something gleamed in the moonlight. A small, silvery glimmer of hope.

"What if we don't have to make a choice?"

Barack narrowed his eyes.

"What if," I continued, "Steve takes Gonzalez back to shore, and you and I take the speedboat over to Caruso's yacht. If we take the speedboat instead of the tour boat, we'd have the element of surprise back in our favor."

"We didn't find their keys."

I winked. "That's because they're still in the ignition."

Barack and I piled into the speedboat without discussing it. In case things went wrong, the less Steve knew, the better. If things went wrong, they would go very wrong.

"You ever drive one of these things?" Barack asked, staring at the controls like Sarah Palin at a teleprompter.

I shot him a sly grin. "Actually, I have."

Barack looked at me skeptically.

"I'm from Delaware," I said, switching seats with Barack and priming the pump. "I know more about boats than Lawrence Welk knew about polka." I turned the key and pushed the throttle into first gear.

"Sounds like the engine's dead," Barack said when nothing happened.

"It's like a lawnmower," I said, standing with one foot on the seat and another on the platform between me and the motor. I yanked the ripcord, then again, and again, until the motor sputtered to life.

I pulled the throttle into reverse and spun the wheel, backing us away from the tour boat. The rope dropped away. As soon as we were free, I laid into the throttle like it owed me money. The speedboat lurched forward, its nose poking up for a brief moment before settling back down. We were off.

"There aren't any life jackets, Joe," Barack hollered as the wind slapped us around.

"You only need a life jacket if you fall overboard," I shouted. Besides, life jackets wouldn't do us much good where we were going.

Not unless they were made of Kevlar.

51

When we were within a hundred yards of Caruso's yacht, I killed the motor. Our momentum, coupled with the tide, carried us toward the boat under the cover of darkness. The clouds had moved on. The stars were out now, and the moon gave us just enough light to see what we were doing. Up close, the yacht was positively ginormous — a leviathan twice as long as the tour boat, and three stories tall. The name on the side read U.S.S. HOPE. At one time, it had been a tribute to Barack Obama. Now, it seemed like a kick in the shin.

Barack held out a hand to stop us from crashing into the hull, and I grabbed the ladder on the swim deck to keep us from drifting away.

"This is our Moby Dick," I said.

"Call me Ishmael," Barack said. "I hope you weren't planning to harpoon Caruso's boat."

"Don't be ridiculous." Then: "Did you find a harpoon on board?"

He shook his head.

"If we were smart, we would have grabbed those semiautomatics."

"So we could go out in a blaze of glory?" he said. "Use your head, Joe."

I opened the storage hold on the speedboat. I was hoping they'd left a gun or two behind. Not to shoot, but to use as props. For a brief moment, I got excited — the hold was filled with bullets. I dug around, however, and found that was all that was in there. Ammunition for guns we didn't have. I pulled out a sash-style belt of ammo.

Barack was still hanging onto the ladder as our boat bobbed up and down. "What are you going to do, wear that across your chest like Rambo?"

"Just listen. You take your shirt off and drape these over your pecs like you're a Christmas tree and these are the lights. See?" I mimed decorating him with the ammo belt. "You stand behind me, like you've got me hostage. You're a cobra. And you've caught yourself a mongoose. Once we're on the yacht, we put the moves on 'em. Good night, nurse!"

We sat in silence as he digested my plan.

"You know what happens when a cobra

and a mongoose fight, Joe?"

"I'm not a zookeeper."

"A mongoose can tear a cobra in half with one snap of its jaws, and a cobra can kill a mongoose with a single poisonous bite. In the wild, they avoid each other because they both know there's a good chance neither of them walks away from the fight."

"Where'd you learn all that? Harvard?"

"NatGeo," he said.

"We've already dispatched two Crooks."

"We had some help."

"I had the situation under control," I said. "Steve almost screwed it all up."

Barack *mmm-hmmmmm*'d.

"So you're saying you want to be the mongoose."

"Were you listening to me?" he said. "That's —"

A loud thunderclap interrupted us. There was no lightning, though. And it sounded closer than any thunder I'd ever heard. The noise was either a car backfiring or a gunshot.

There weren't any cars on Lake Michigan.

52

Barack used his limber arms to hold the speedboat close as I stuck out a foot onto the ladder. The railing was cold and wet, and the metal slippery as an eel. Once I got a foothold, I was able to hoist myself up.

"Now, Joe, be careful —"

Before Barack could say any more, I was scaling the ladder. Three stories to the top. That was all. I didn't look down, because to look down was to invite trouble. When I was a kid, I'd climbed a construction worker's ladder in the freezing rain to the top of the skeleton of a new building six stories high — fifty or more feet in the air. Never once looked down. That was the key. I'd seen more than one of my classmates end up flat on their back or worse due to vertigo.

At the top of the ladder, I caught my breath. I looked left and right. The coast was clear. There was shouting coming from the bow — a man's voice. Barking orders.

"You OK?" Barack asked from below.

I looked down. Instinct. He was right behind me. Our eyes met, and then the vertigo kicked in. The boat bobbed up and down. The roasted peanuts were swirling in my stomach, like a tornado building itself from the ground up.

I tumbled over the railing and landed on the deck, shoulder first. I rolled over onto my back. Barack quickly followed, taking the more standard tactic of climbing over the railing one leg at a time.

"I tied up the boat," Barack said, kneeling beside me. "You don't look so hot."

He placed a hand on my chest. The stars were spinning above me. I had to get my bearings, and fast. It wouldn't be long before we'd be discovered.

Breathe, he was saying. *Nice, steady breaths . . . In, out . . . In, out . . .*

I brushed his arm away. "We don't have time for yoga."

"It's called mindful meditation. Being aware of your breathing is one of the easiest ways to clear your mind and be more present in your daily life. I can send you a link to the app I use —"

"Later," I said. He helped me to my feet. The vertigo left as fast as it had come on. We crept low, under the cabin windows,

314

toward the voice I'd heard. The voice that had gone silent.

I peeked around the cabin. In the moonlight, I could make out a couple of sun chairs. An end table. A few half-empty cocktail glasses. It was a lounge area. Deserted.

No, not quite.

There was a lifeless man in a checkered suit jacket, splayed out on his back.

Caruso.

Dark red soaked through his shirt near the collar. The spot was small as a dime, but that was all it took. I tried to look everywhere except for his eyes, but it was impossible to look away. They were open, staring straight up at the stars, unblinking. He was gazing into the infinite.

Barack knelt beside him. The president was known for keeping his emotions in check, but he was a human being. A human being whose friend had been taken from him by a single gunshot. I could feel the anger rising off him like heat. His bottom lip was trembling.

I felt a hard poke in my lower back. I didn't have to turn around to know it was the barrel of a gun.

"Move," a voice said. I glanced back to get a glimpse of my new friend. It was another young man, this one barrel-chested and wearing Crooks' colors. It was like they rolled them off an assembly line.

He nudged me again, pushing me forward. I stumbled toward Barack, who caught me.

I had a sinking feeling in my gut. Somebody had wanted to get the two of us far from the Secret Service. They knew the only way to do that was to trick us into thinking we'd come up with the idea ourselves. All they needed was to convince us that there was nobody we could trust in the city. That we had to do this alone.

Suddenly, it all came together in my head. Shaun had been abducted from the hospital by a big man. Barack and I had both assumed "big" as in "tall," since there was no video to verify the man's identity. What if the receptionist had meant "big" as in "the size of a refrigerator"?

Bento Box was waiting for us on the other side of the cabin. Despite the bandage wrapped around his head, Rahm's fixer had a confident, self-satisfied look on his face. Another armed young man flanked him, decked out in silver and black.

"If you're here for Caruso's TED Talk, it's been canceled," Bento Box said. "Welcome to his DEAD Talk."

53

The storage hold under the deck was filled with dozens of cardboard boxes. One was open. In the dim light, I could see an Uzi inside, an automatic weapon I'd only seen in movies. There were a few extra clips in the box. I already knew the rest of the boxes contained more exotic weaponry — I'd seen the manifest of missing guns. There were enough boxes here to fill a shipping container.

Bento Box led us through the storage area to a closet, where, gagged and handcuffed to an exposed pipe, sat Shaun Denton. His lips were cracked, bleeding. There was a hospital bracelet on his wrist.

"Why keep him like this?" I asked.

"He's a bargaining chip. I was hoping we could all come to some sort of deal. Would you rather I tossed him overboard with his wheelchair?"

"I'd rather see him in the hospital," I said.

"Why do you guys care about this kid? His own family wouldn't care if he went on a permanent vacation," Bento Box said. "His aunt's too strung out half the time to know where he's at, and the rest of the time she's working for eight bucks an hour to keep the lights on. Did she go see him in the hospital?"

I didn't say anything. Shaun's eyes fluttered open and closed. He was still partially sedated.

"You're beginning to see how things are, Joe," the fixer said. "This isn't Delaware. This isn't some peace-and-love hippie commune where the only currency is maple syrup."

"You're thinking of Vermont."

"Which one is Delaware?"

"The First State," I said, puffing my chest up. "Our number one export is dairy milk."

"Since we're talking trivia, tell me something: Why didn't you tell me your boy here was part of the Rising Stars program? When I asked how you knew him, you acted like you'd forgotten how to speak English all of a sudden."

Barack was being suspiciously quiet. I hoped that he was trying to calculate a way out of our predicament, and not simply trying to bottle up his anger. If he went supernova, would I be able to contain him?

"Shaun's a victim in all of this," I said. "Let him go, and then we can talk."

Bento Box wagged a finger at us. "Shaun's been a bad, bad boy. He knew how lax security was around the freight yard. Tell me: Where do you think the Red Door gets all those donations from?"

"The community," I said. I couldn't look at Shaun, because I knew where this was going.

"And where does the community get box after box of canned goods and electronics and whatever else falls out of a jimmied shipping container? *Thou shalt not steal from thy neighbor* doesn't apply when it's from a boxcar passing through your town, apparently. Pastor Brown knows all the shipments are insured, so who's he hurting? His boys know how to work crowbars."

Barack's expression was pained. Was he realizing how few options we had, or was the fixer getting to him? Shaun looked away when I finally looked his way.

I didn't need Shaun to confirm that what Bento Box was saying was true. I could see how the burglary had gone down now. Shaun had helped his fellow juvenile ex-cons plot the heist. How many times they'd pulled similar jobs was anyone's guess. This time, they'd broken into two containers before hitting the jackpot. In the third container they found the weapons.

"Stealing canned goods and electronics was one thing. But the kids, including Shaun, knew Pastor Brown wouldn't approve of them taking those guns. Couldn't tell him. They also knew they needed to stash the guns somewhere until the heat blew over. Couldn't hide them in a storage unit or in some homeboy's pad. Somebody would talk. Somebody would rip them off."

"So they went to Caruso."

Bento Box patted a support beam. "They saw the yacht as a floating stash house. Even if someone found out the guns were here, who would dare rip off an OG like Caruso? They fed him some BS about the church doing a charity drive, one of those gun buyback programs. He wasn't an idiot, of course. Saw right through it. But he also thought that if the guns were on his boat, then they weren't in the community. He knew the kids were looking for some way to unload the guns, but it was going to take weeks. Months. I suppose he planned to reason with them when the time came. Unfortunately for him, his time came first."

I'd known it from the moment I'd seen his body on the deck. That didn't make it

any less painful to hear.
   Caruso was innocent.

54

I felt like I'd been hit by an elevated train. Barack had a similarly shocked look on his face.

Bento Box laughed. "Don't look so surprised."

"He was at the freight yard this morning," I said, as if that could justify how wrong we'd been.

"Caruso gave your boy Shaun a ride to work. Probably lecturing him the whole time, too." He ran his fingers over the Uzi like he was petting a cat. "Trying to get him to do the right thing. What he didn't know was that Shaun had already tried to 'do the right thing.'"

"I don't get it," I said.

"I do," Barack said, breaking his long silence. "He'd gone to the police. He'd turned on his crew, because of what happened to his mother."

The fixer's eyebrows went up. "Winner

winner, chicken dinner. Shaun talked to a neighborhood cop he knew through the Red Door. The cop must have been all re-assuring, telling him nobody would ever know who had reported the heist, blah blah blah."

"Liar," Shaun mumbled. "He was a liar."

The cop wrote up his report so that it looked like the kid was fingering the Crooks, Bento Box explained. The cop was a member of the Red Door and didn't want to make trouble for Pastor Brown. The report may have been marked CONFIDENTIAL, but nothing stays confidential in this town. The cop knew that much. He was thinking ahead, trying to work the angles. Trying to see how he could cut himself a piece of the pie. "Someone inside the department tipped me off to the report. You don't win the lottery without paying taxes, so when I went to collect from the Crooks, imagine their surprise. The cop broke down in my hands pretty fast and admitted what was what."

I watched Bento Box crack his knuckles. "And the gang member who shot Shaun, Kendrick. The one who was killed in the car accident . . ."

"I wasn't the only one who'd got hold of the cop's informant report. Somebody must have slipped the Crooks a copy. As the saying goes, snitches get stitches. Especially lying snitches. That's also why they lent me a few boys to help out with this operation."

There was another reason they were helping, I realized. Caruso was a former Crook. The gang couldn't stand that he'd made it out, that he'd made something of himself. He might have been respected in the old neighborhood, but that didn't mean the Crooks wouldn't take him out if given the chance.

I could see where Benny Polaski was going with this. He kept his hands clean. It was almost certain that one of the Crooks had put the bullet in Caruso's chest. The fixer had kidnapped Shaun, but that was only because Kendrick had so thoroughly bungled his assassination attempt — first, he'd let Shaun live, and second, he'd been spooked away from the hospital by our presence in the parking garage. By then, Barack and I were involved. Shaun had more value alive than dead.

A bargaining chip. My stomach turned at the thought. What's more, Bento Box knew he could demand almost anything from us in exchange for Shaun. He had us over a barrel.

The second foot soldier, who'd stayed behind on the deck, burst into the room, rifle slung over his shoulder.

"There's a boat," he said.

Bento Box turned to him. "And?"

"A Coast Guard boat."

Bento Box narrowed his eyes at us. This wasn't part of his plan. I believed he had his own contacts within the police department that he'd trusted to steer law enforcement away from Caruso's yacht. The Feds were out of his price range, apparently.

"Did you do something stupid?" he spat at us.

I hadn't called the Coast Guard. Neither had Barack. Maybe Steve had, though the timing was off.

"Let me go up and talk to them," I said.

"You're crazy," Bento Box said. Barack also shot me a worried look. Whatever plan he'd been trying to cook up had obviously been blown to holy heck by the arrival of the Coast Guard.

"I don't want to see anyone else get hurt," I said. "I'll go up and let whoever's in the boat know it's all a misunderstanding. They're here for us, not for you. Not for your guns. I tell them everything's jolly as a green giant. You let us take Shaun. We never speak about any of this ever again. Nobody goes to jail. Nobody dies."

The gun-toting Crooks were watching

Bento Box with anticipation, waiting for orders. They were young and dumb, fueled by lethal cocktails of testosterone and adrenaline. Their boss had more self-control. He knew that if a firefight broke out, the safest place to be wasn't on a boat carrying half a ton of live ammunition.

"Take him upstairs," he ordered, and then turned to me. "Get rid of the Feds. Not a word about the guns. When you return, then we'll start bargaining. I'm going to stay down here with your friends. An insurance policy."

Barack stared at me. *We don't have much choice,* he said with his eyes. *It's not just my life on the line. It's Shaun's. Do what the man wants.*

It's a lot to say with one's eyes, but Barack and I had known each other for a long time. We didn't need words to communicate.

55

I was led to the cabin, where the yacht's captain was waiting. He was dressed in a white shirt, decorated with navy blue shoulder patches. His long blond hair was slicked back. I assumed he was Caruso's man, and in the same position as the rest of us hostages.

"They're telling us to follow them back to shore," the captain said. He sounded Australian.

Through the window, I could see the American flag flying off the back of the Coast Guard boat. They were twenty yards from the yacht. Close enough that I could see several figures in black moving about the deck. They were getting ready to board us.

I picked up the CB radio. "This is Joseph Robinette Biden Jr. Who am I talking to?"

"Did you say 'Joe Biden'?"

"That's right. What's your name, fella?"

He told me his name, which went in one ear and out the other. A nobody. He wasn't with the Coast Guard — he was with the Bureau of Alcohol, Tobacco, and Firearms. The Crook and the captain exchanged worried looks. The ATF weren't your go-to federal branch for presidential welfare check-ups. The situation had suddenly become much more complicated. Thankfully, I'd taken an improv class at the University of Delaware.

"You need to listen to me, and listen carefully. I don't know who sent you, but there's been a mix-up. President Obama and I are fine."

The CB squawked. "President Obama?"

"That's what I said."

The Crook was watching me closely. He'd left his rifle downstairs, but his hand was on the butt of a pistol stuffed into his waistband.

"Enough monkey business," the ATF agent said. "We're giving you one chance to comply: Follow us back to shore, or we'll board your vessel."

The Crook and the captain were looking at me, waiting to follow my lead. The ATF were here for the weapons cache. A firefight was imminent. Especially once they noticed the dead man on the deck. I needed to buy us some time.

"We're not going anywhere," I said. "And if you government thugs set one foot on this boat without a warrant, there's going to be some serious consequences."

"We've got a warrant," the agent said. "We'll need to board to show it to you —"

"That ain't how it's going to work. Fax it over, and we'll take a look at it."

"Fax?"

"You heard me." I let my finger off the CB button and turned to the captain. "Do you have a fax machine on this yacht?"

He shook his head.

"Good," I whispered.

I got back on the CB. "I'm going to give you a fax number. You ready?"

There was no reply. Only silence.

Then, the agent spoke up: "We don't have a fax machine."

"Then I suppose you're going to have to find one," I said.

56

Barack's head emerged from the stairwell right as the Crook was escorting me back from the cabin. There was a moment of confusion on all of our parts — we knew the game had changed, but none of us were entirely sure who had come out ahead.

"Where's Bento?" the Crook asked, waving his handgun around. One wrong move and somebody was going to get some ballistic therapy.

Barack ignored him. "We don't have much time," he said, stepping onto the deck. He reached back into the stairwell and pulled Shaun up. The kid was moving around well for somebody who'd taken a couple of slugs that morning. St. Paddy had come through with some luck o' the Irish for him.

The Crook dropped his gun. At first, I thought he was just showing respect for our forty-fourth president, but then I saw what he'd spotted.

Barack held a grenade in his right hand.

"I bought us some time," he said. He went to the railing and scanned the empty waters. "Um, Joe. Where's the Coast Guard?"

"I also bought us some time."

"You were supposed to keep the Coast Guard here to arrest Polaski and his crew. I picked up this grenade as we passed the open boxes of weapons to use as leverage to free Shaun. Right before you went up the stairs, we made eye contact, and I thought I made it clear that I had things under control. Instead, you sent the Coast Guard away — which was exactly what Polaski asked you to do."

"You just looked at me and waggled your eyebrows. In what language does that mean, 'I've got a grenade so hold the boat'?"

I glanced at the Crook backed up against the cabin wall. He was shaking in his gym shoes. He might not have seen a grenade before, but he knew what one could do. If Barack pulled that pin, in three seconds our limbs would be raining down on Lake Michigan.

"We'll take the speedboat," Barack said. "Why don't we radio the Coast Guard, get them to turn back around. We need to make sure the Crooks don't dump the guns. Where's the radio?"

I motioned to the cabin door. I could see the captain at the controls through one of the portside windows. He was preoccupied with a bottle of whiskey.

"I'll hold down the deck while you hop on the radio," Barack said. "Rahm's meathead and the other Crook are still downstairs. I don't know how long the rope will hold — he's right behind me, isn't he?" Barack said.

I nodded. "What kind of knot did you use?"

"There's more than one type of knot?"

Where was Steve when we needed him?

Bento Box plucked the grenade from Barack's hand. Like taking candy from a baby. "Move," he said, marching us to the bow of the boat. The Crooks followed close behind.

"This boy needs medical attention," Barack said. His arm was wrapped around Shaun's shoulders. The more he moved, the greater the chance his wounds would reopen. There was a reason he'd been sedated in the hospital.

"Keep walking," Bento Box said.

He marched us to the front of the deck, where we stopped. We'd passed the spot where Caruso's body had been. Had they dumped him overboard?

"Keep going," the fixer barked.

He wanted us to jump. Apparently the offer to bargain had been pulled. While the air had warmed today, it would take weeks of higher temps before the frigid lake caught up. The spray from the motorboat had been enough to chill me to the fillings in my teeth. If an expert swimmer like Steve could only last a few moments in the water, what chance did we have? Within thirty seconds, our limbs would be numb. Useless. There would be no treading water to keep ourselves alive. No swimming to shore.

I looked over my shoulder. Bento Box was five yards away, next to the wet bar.

"Move," a hoarse voice said.

I spun around. Shaun, propped up against Barack, held a black pistol in his trembling right hand. He was struggling to hold his arm steady. The Crooks raised their guns in response.

I was caught in the middle.

"Where'd you get that?" I asked Shaun.

Tears were streaming down his face. If we lived because Shaun pulled the trigger and took out the madman and his goons, would that make him a hero? Or just another victim who had succumbed to the same violent cycle he'd fought so hard to escape?

"This isn't the way," Barack said, cradling

Shaun, trying to disarm him without dis-
charging the gun. "This isn't the way."

Shaun relaxed his grip and Barack took
the weapon. But instead of kicking it aside,
Barack raised it in my direction. I was
between him and his targets. Neither side
could get a clean shot off with me in the
way. "Step aside, Joe."

Nobody breathed.

Bento Box plucked the pin from the
grenade. His bodyguards, figuring out their
new business partner was off his Cracker
Barrel rocker, swiftly abandoned him, rush-
ing below deck. I attributed the fixer's er-
ratic behavior to the head injury he'd
sustained earlier in front of Tribune Tower.
Of course, I'd been knocked around some
today, too. We were all trying to tough it
out.

"Who wants to be the hero?" Bento Box
said. He was grinning, taunting us. "Can't
pull the trigger, Mr. President? What about
you, Joe — want to take a swing at me?
Didn't think so. This is where your white
savior fantasy comes to an end."

His sausage-like fingers were wrapped
around the grenade. If he relaxed his grip,
the spring-loaded striker would spark the
cap. The fuse would burn down and the
grenade would explode, sending fragments

in every direction. Barack hadn't been crazy enough to pull the pin — he'd been bluffing. This madman didn't know the meaning of the word "bluff."

I gritted my teeth and balled my fists. Using force was a last resort, but, in Barack's own words, force was sometimes necessary. *Using force is a recognition of the imperfections of man and the limits of reason,* he'd once said.

We'd reached the limits of reason.

57

Before I could move or Barack could take a shot, Caruso came charging from out of nowhere, armed with a folded deck chair. He let out a Ric Flair "Woooo!" as he struck Bento Box across the back with a wicked chair-shot. The grenade popped out of the fixer's hand and skittered away, still live. Compared to my younger days at Archmere, I wasn't so explosive out of the gate.

Before I could reach it the grenade veered off to the left, coming to a rest underneath one of the reclined sunbathing chairs. Nowhere near its intended targets. Not that it mattered. When it blew, it would tear through everyone on deck just the same. Like Pa Biden used to say, *Close only counts in horseshoes and hand grenades.*

I'd never played around with explosive munitions, but I had plenty of experience with horseshoes.

I also had plenty of experience with

another sport: football. Back in high school, they called me "Hands." I could catch anything thrown my way. Offense or defense. Less well known was that I could also throw the ball. I didn't just have hands; I had arms, too.

"Joe!" Barack shouted, shielding Shaun from the imminent explosion. His voice was far away. Out of the corner of my eye, I saw Bento Box staggering around, hands to his own throat, face purple. He was choking on something. A Werther's. He must have swallowed the hard candy when Caruso hit him. There was no time for the Heimlich, however.

The soles of Barack's dress shoes hadn't been made for ten-meter dashes on decks slick with rain. I skidded to a stop, tipping backward and landing on my unpadded keister. I felt under the chair for the grenade. It was like unhooking a bra one-handed at a drive-in. Only difference was that the coming explosion would be of a very different sort if I failed.

There. I had it.

Only one way to do this. No time to stand and set my feet properly. I had to throw it from my knees, like an NFL quarterback desperately trying to rid himself of a ball he'd fumbled and recovered. Although I wasn't trying to reach an open receiver, I still needed to throw a Hail Mary. Get it all the way to the end zone from deep in my own territory.

I reared back and chucked the grenade into the sky, aiming for the stars and praying I could hit the moon.

Maybe that was a bit too much to ask from an arm that hadn't seen much action in the past five decades besides backyard touch-football matches at Biden family gatherings.

The grenade barely cleared the railing.

I heard it plunk into the lake and —

KA-BLOOEY.

The boat rocked back and forth, flinging me from side to side. Water shot up in a geyser, high into the air. It rained down on the deck with a terrifying splash, drenching me. Chilling me to the bone.

When things had settled, I made my way over to Barack. Shaun was leaning on the railing. Struggling against the sedative in his system. Caruso was on his back. Legs elevated. Not nearly as dead as he'd appeared to be when we boarded the yacht. This was a very good thing because Caruso and Shaun had been the heroes of the day — not Barack Obama, not Joe Biden. My ears were ringing, but I was in one piece.

"Which way did Bento Box go?"

"He went overboard and never surfaced," Barack said. "We're close enough to shore. He'll wash up later this spring."

I shook my head. I'd been trying to prevent more bloodshed. I didn't know if Barack had planned to pull the trigger, or if the only thing that stopped him was Caruso's intervention. I didn't know if even he knew. All I knew was that we would never talk about it — not with each other, not with the ATF or the police. Not with anyone.

Barack limped to the railing and peered over. "I don't want to alarm you, Joe, but you blew a hole in the side of the yacht."

"How big of a hole?"

"You ever seen *Titanic*?"

"We'll take the speedboat."

He shook his head and pointed toward the shore in the distance. The speedboat was being piloted by the drunken Australian captain, his long blond hair flowing behind him.

I looked over the railing on the other side, where Bento Box had tumbled overboard while choking. The water was black, impenetrable. Except for the white caps lit up by the moon, there was nothing bobbing on its surface. Nobody crying out for help. Nobody but the dead.

"Do you hear that?" Barack said.

My ears were still ringing, but I could hear something else now. A dull roar. My tie whipped to the side. We looked up to see a rope ladder unfurling from the sky . . .

58

The police helicopter dropped Barack and me off on shore. Moments later, the ambulatory chopper flew overhead with Shaun and Caruso, en route to St. Bernard's. Caruso would be in surgery soon but had told us it wasn't the first time he'd been shot. He'd live. Shaun, too. The kid would undergo several more days of intravenous antibiotics, but he was a fighter. I knew now that Pastor Brown had been right. It wasn't his time.

I also knew that Pastor Brown was going to have to answer some tough questions. I wanted to believe that he hadn't known what the kids in his church had been up to, that Bento Box had been lying. I wanted to believe he would continue to feed the community and be a guiding light. Ultimately, I didn't have a place in the conversation. Barack did. Their friendship would be tested in ways that ours never had and never would, God willing.

Rahm parted the sea of cops and medical personnel who'd surrounded us. He welcomed us back to the land of the living. "Michelle reached me at home. Said she received a strange call from an ATF agent who asked if her number accepted faxes. They discovered pretty quickly what was going on, and how all the pieces fit. That's when I put together the rescue operation."

"You gave them Michelle's number," Barack said. "Good thinking."

I grinned. I had a few tricks up my sleeve.

"I'm just glad you're both safe," Rahm said. "Michelle said that if something happened to either one of you in my town, I wouldn't have to answer to the Feds — I'd have to answer to her."

Barack smiled. "I married up, what can I say?"

"Did you run into the Secret Service agent we sent back on the tour boat?" I asked.

Rahm nodded. "He had a couple of guys giftwrapped for us. Said you might have some more presents out there."

Right now, the police were salvaging what they could from the sinking yacht. The two Crooks were in custody. If the serial numbers on the recovered weapons matched the missing guns, it was going to be a big coup for Chicago PD. There'd been an ongoing joint investigation into the burglary between the city and the ATF. The bust would give the city bragging rights over the Feds. Rahm told us he'd keep our names out of it, for what it was worth. That wasn't for our benefit. His office would decide who got to take credit for the bust. It was another favor in a city built on favors.

"Now you can finally tell that leprechaun to quit following me around," I told him.

"Leprechaun?"

"Little guy, green jacket. Green hat. The guy you put on me to keep tabs so that I wouldn't get into trouble."

He shook his head. "The guy Benny put on you was a real grabowski. Had a mustache like a muskrat on his upper lip."

"Mike Ditka."

"That's him all right."

"He picked me up in a cab from the airport, and then I saw him again and . . . Dang it. I got snookered. So who's the leprechaun?"

"Hell if I know, Joe," Rahm said. He apologized for everything that Benny Polaski had put me through and promised to keep the police chief's feet to the coals until they'd rooted out the web of corruption we'd uncovered. I believed he had no idea that his fixer had been running a clandestine criminal empire out of City Hall, but it was a tall order to kick over every rock in Chicago. If you did that, would there be a city left?

Rahm shook my hand and told me to keep in touch. We both knew that wouldn't be happening. We finally trusted each other, though, and that was reason for mild celebration.

I turned to the city skyline. It was nearing two in the morning. The beat reporters would be tabulating the day's body count right about now. With any luck, the snakes had been driven back into hiding by the storm. Tomorrow would be another day, though. Violence would again rear its ugly head. Crime was baked into the city's DNA. The same was also true for the entire country. We could keep working toward a more perfect union, but there was blood in the soil. Blood of Native Americans. Blood of slaves. Blood of a war that had pitted brother against brother. We were still paying the price. Even knowing all that, however, I wasn't about to throw up my arms. I wasn't about to give up.

"Forward," I said.

Barack looked at me sideways. "What's that?"

"Our campaign slogan, from 2012. For-ward. We keep moving forward, even if the current keeps pushing us back." I paused. "I'm paraphrasing from *The Great Gatsby.*"

"I've read it."

"I suppose you have. Ready to hit the hay?"

"I'm tired as hell, but I've got all this energy," he said. "I feel like I could hit a rope line for an hour of handshakes."

"You think Jeni's is open this late?"

"Isn't it a little cold for ice cream?"

The weather had cooled off some follow-ing the storm, true. But "too cold" for ice cream? There was no such thing as bad weather for ice cream. Not even snake weather.

59

There was no line for the Centennial Wheel. Navy Pier was closed, but Rahm had made a call and the ride was now lit up and waiting for me and Barack. Just the two of us. We even had our ice cream — off-brand Shamrock Shakes from the only open ice cream shop at this hour, Pee-Wee Penguin's Ice Cream Igloo. Not my first choice, but, as they say, any fort in a storm.

The enormous Ferris wheel lurched into action. I waved to the agents as the ride slowly took us up, up, up, until they were nothing more than ants in sunglasses. A seagull flew past the floor-to-ceiling window on our cabin, causing me to shriek.

Barack laughed. "You're not afraid of heights, are you, Joe?"

The fingers of my free hand were dug deep into the armrests. "I had my own airplane, if you don't remember. Air Force Two."

He nodded. We both knew that flying on an airplane was one thing; hitching a ride on a carnival contraption was quite another. For sheer terror, however, it was no match for Funland's Haunted Mansion.

I looked out over the lake, which stretched for miles and miles — so far, in fact, that even during the daylight you couldn't see the other shore. Waves were crashing against the rocks lining the pier as flocks of seagulls scattered and came back together. Bento Box's body hadn't been found.

I slurped the last bit of my shake. "I didn't know you knew Pig Latin."

He laughed. "Did I say something in Pig Latin?"

"We were tied up at the Alley, and you said *ixnay* —"

"*Ixnay* on our *ames-nay.*"

"You know how long it's been since I've heard that? God, it would have to have been back in Scranton." I shook my head. "It's the only foreign language I ever learned, you know. They didn't teach us Spanish back then. I know you can speak Filipino, and Swahili, and all that."

"I don't know a word of Filipino, Joe. Not a word."

"No? I could have sworn that's what Rahm told me."

"Blaming it on Rahm, OK. OK, Joe."

Our cabin reached the tip-top of the wheel. The skyscraper windows in the Loop twinkled emerald like a hundred thousand jewels.

"I'm going to have to reschedule my flight," I told Barack. "Jill's waiting to hear back from me."

"Michelle called her — it's all good. We're dropping you off tomorrow afternoon on the way back to DC."

"What do you have, a private jet these days?"

"Actually, we do, Joe."

"Must be nice," I mumbled.

"Hey, don't be that way — you could be back up in Air Force One before you know it." He paused. "If that's what you want. What is it that you want, exactly?"

"You know, I wasn't sure when I came to town. I was exhausted. Beat down by the road. But when I heard Oprah was at the forum, it awoke something in me. Y'know, I've watched everyone and their mother jump into the primary race. Hasn't fazed me. Not one bit. This was different, though. The prospect of coming face-to-face with a potential rival got my competitive juices flowing. I'm not asking you to endorse me during the primaries or anything, I know how tricky it is —"

"It is."

"— but I also know that I've still got that fighting spirit. *To those whom much is given, much is asked.* I can't right every wrong, but we left things unfinished. There's still work to do. If there's somebody better, by God, let's go toe to toe in the ring and may the best man or woman win. And if there truly is somebody better, then best of luck to them, but they're going to have to fight me. If I go down, I'm going down swinging."

He studied me, seemingly pleased at the fire I was able to muster after all we'd been through in the past seventeen hours. "You know that once you're president, we can finally talk about Roswell together."

"What did you tell that record store guy?"

"Exactly what you'll learn after you're sworn in as president." He smiled. Not a grin, but an honest-to-God genuine smile. He held a fist out to me. "Good luck, Joe."

I jabbed at him, grazing his knuckles.

"You're going to have to work on your fist-bumps, Joe."

"Can't we just shake hands?"

"Spreads germs," Barack said. "Plus, fist-bumps are cool. Shaking hands isn't."

"You think I could be a cool president."

"Joe."

I winked at him and he shook his head. We both knew I'd never be a cool president. Heck, I might never be an uncool president — there were nearly nine months between now and Iowa's first-in-the-nation caucus. Plenty of time to mull my decision some more. Who knew what the future held for me? As I'd learned long ago, fate has a strange way of intervening. If I did run, however, the first campaign hire would be a decent fist-bump coach.

60

Barack looked both ways for traffic and dashed across the street, a new Secret Service agent in tow. Steve had already left to visit his parents. He'd had enough lunacy for one weekend. I almost felt bad he hadn't stuck around. The little guy was starting to grow on me. Barack and I weren't on the lam this time — in fact, we'd just finished a late breakfast of green eggs and potato pancakes and were headed to Barack's old barbershop.

I was still exhausted. All night long, I'd replayed the day's events in my head, from beginning to end, wondering what I could have done differently. If there was more I could have done for Shaun. At the butt-crack of dawn, I'd hopped a cab to the hospital. He'd made it through surgery. His aunt was there by his side, holding his hand. They were both asleep. Shaun had been wrong when he'd told me no one would walk two blocks for him. His aunt — whatever problems she had — had come through for him. Caruso had come through for him. Shaun had more family than he realized. I'd handed the receptionist my Ray-Bans. She promised to give them to the kid when he woke up.

Barack held the barbershop door open as I caught up to him. SMITTY'S, a neon sign in the window announced. There was an old-fashioned red, white, and blue striped pole out front that was cracked down the side.

"If you're gonna come in, come in," a booming baritone shouted from inside. "Hot air ain't free."

It was in the forties outside, but inside the barbershop it was sweltering. There was even a fan running. The walls were decorated with framed Bears and White Sox posters. I spotted a Muhammad Ali poster identical to the one Barack had had in the West Wing.

Six pairs of dark eyes stared at me like I'd stepped out of a spaceship. They were all men my age or older seated along a wall in folding chairs. Not getting haircuts, just hanging out.

"Barry Obama," an older black man in a barber's jacket said. His beard was as gray as the hair on Barack's head. "I'll be damned."

Barack embraced him in a tight hug. "It's been too long, Smitty."

The barber ran his fingers through Barack's buzzed locks. "You been cutting this yourself?"

"Got me a guy in DC."

"What's his name?"

"You don't know him."

Smitty narrowed his eyes.

"Jerry," Barack said. "Jerry Feinstein."

"Take a seat."

Barack nodded in my direction. "Think you could do my friend, too? Shave and a haircut."

Smitty looked over at the burly Service agent standing by the door, and then looked me up and down. "Two bodyguards? I'll be damned."

I was about to go on a good ol'-fashioned rant, but Barack slapped the back of a maroon barber's chair. "He's just messing with you, Joe," he said. "Let's get you cleaned up."

We took seats next to each other, facing the mirrors along the wall. Smitty pinned a paper bib around each of our necks and disappeared into the back room for his clippers.

"So what's going to happen now?" I whispered to Barack. "Are our chairs going to whisk us through the floor and into an underground tunnel? What are we *really* here for?"

"What's going to happen," he said, "is we're going to get our hair cut. We've been through some real-life shit these past twenty-four hours, Joe. You want to go home to Jill looking like you closed down the bars with me last night?"

I ran a hand over the scruff on my chin.

"I used to write stories in this place," Barack said. He tapped the side of his head. "Up here, when I was getting my hair cut. Smitty doesn't do much talking. Not while he's working."

That was a relief. My vocal cords needed the rest.

In the mirror, I watched as a Crown Victoria pulled up across the street. The same make and model that had tailed us on the Dan Ryan the previous day. The driver hopped out to feed the meter. He was wearing a green newsboy cap and jacket.

The leprechaun.

I leaped up and ran out the door, bib flapping over my shoulder like a cape. The leprechaun saw me coming and spilled his change. There was no time to get back into his car, so he took off down the sidewalk.

I ran into traffic, dodging cars as they whipped around me. "Hold up!" I screamed at the wee man, who was holding onto his hat to keep it from sailing off his head. There was no way I was letting him get away this time.

He ducked into an alley. By the time I rounded the corner, there was no sign of him. His trail had gone cold. The alley was too long for him to have run the whole thing — a good city block — in the second or two it'd taken me to reach him. He had to be . . . there. A dumpster, its lid closed. A decent hiding place, except for one thing: dumpsters don't pray.

"Mother Mary, who art in heaven . . ."

I lifted the lid. The guy was huddling amongst the trash bags, shaking and saying prayers to St. Mary and anyone else he could think of.

"Come on out," I said. "I'm not going to hurt you."

He looked up at me. I backed off to give him space, and — perhaps because he believed me, or perhaps because he knew he'd been caught and there was nowhere to hide — he climbed out.

Up close, he wasn't as short as I'd thought, and the bright green jacket was actually more of a forest color. Likewise, his red beard was more strawberry blond, with flecks of gray.

"Start talking, pal. And no blarney."

He sheepishly handed me a business card. "Michael O'Rearden, freelance reporter," I read out loud. "So, what, you've been following me around town looking for a scoop, is that it?"

He looked up, into the clouds breaking up the blue sky. "I've got one helluva scoop. Picture this: Joe Biden — amateur detective. Racing around the city in a Trans Am with his pal Barack Obama, trying to solve a crime that the police have given up on."

"Sounds far-fetched."

"We'll see what the *Sun-Times* says. Or maybe the *Washington Post*? Look out, Woodward and Bumstein — I'm coming for your Pulitzers."

"It sounds a lot like that novel that just came out."

He narrowed his eyes. "Novel? What novel?"

"Check out your local independent bookstore before you go any further with your 'story.' And next time, come up with something original, kid."

"But I saw —" He paused, flustered, then patted his jacket. "Where is it? I had the evidence right here . . . My phone. Where's my phone?"

"Joe!" a muffled voice shouted.

Barack rounded the corner, his bib still attached around his neck. I realized mine was, too — we must have looked like a couple of fools. I began to laugh, partly out of the lunacy of the situation, and partly due to exhaustion.

"What are you doing, Joe? Dumpster diving?" Barack asked. His agent jogged to meet us. Steve would have never been that far behind.

"I caught him. I finally caught him."

"Caught who?"

"The leprechaun," I said. "Well, he's not really a leprechaun, because there's no such thing, but . . ." I swiveled around and saw that the guy had disappeared again. Impossible. Had he climbed through a window somewhere, or scaled one of the brick two-story buildings like a squirrel?

Barack peered into the dumpster. "A leprechaun, eh? Looks like he led you straight to his treasure, Joe."

Were leprechauns real? Had I been bamboozled? Grandpappy had sworn he'd seen them all the time back in Ireland. Of course, he was only three when his family had immigrated to the United States. Three-year-olds were, historically, full of malarkey.

Barack pulled a phone out of the trash. "Some treasure, huh?"

His BlackBerry.

Or, rather, the reporter's.

We'd already found Barack's phone — Caruso had turned it in to the Lost and Found at the Tribune Tower last night, just prior to heading upstairs to the reception. A change of shift meant building security hadn't realized whose phone it was. That's where it sat until the Secret Service discovered it this morning.

"What is it about BlackBerries and Chicagoans?" I said, snatching the reporter's phone from Barack's hands. "And you say I'm the one with an old phone."

"It's the security," Barack said. "Even law enforcement can't crack them."

I glared at him. "Maybe if everyone quit doing shady stuff up in here, you could all use normal phones."

I still had the leprechaun's business card. I'd drop the phone in the mail, along with a note asking him to spend his time on something more newsworthy than Joe Biden. Something like the five hundred murders a year in his city, most of which went unsolved. Somebody needed to tell their stories. I wouldn't erase any of his photos — not that I could if I'd wanted to, if what Barack was saying was true. That didn't mean I was sending it Priority.

"You got anything going on tonight that you have to be in DC for?" I asked Barack. "Because if you don't, there's going to be a little get-together at my place."

"Sunday dinner with the Bidens? I wouldn't miss it for the world, Joe." He slapped me on the back. "You want to invite Oprah?"

I scowled at him. Playfully, but also not. I wasn't worried about her running for president any longer. But I also knew that if we were spotted together, the speculation would begin that I was casting around for a potential running mate. It was a little early in the game for that kind of talk.

I rang Jill and told her the good news. "Mama, I'm coming home."

"What are you bringing me? It'd better be something good."

Barack had been right — leave your wife for a couple of weeks, you'd better bring home a souvenir. Luckily for me, I had just the thing. I fished the baseball-bat pen out of my pocket. I'd forgotten to hand it back to the undercover cop after I signed his book.

"You'll never guess what it is," I said.

"It's not some cheap souvenir you picked up at the airport, is it?"

"It's a long story," I said. "About that surprise party this evening, you mind if I bring along a couple of friends?"

Before she could respond, I corrected myself.

"Sorry, not friends." I glanced at Barack. "I meant family."

ACKNOWLEDGMENTS

Thank you to my editor at Quirk Books, Jhanteigh Kupihea; the Quirk Books team in Philadelphia, including Brett Cohen, Nicole De Jackmo, Moneka Hewlett, Rebecca Gyllenhaal, Jane Morley, Mary Ellen Wilson, Ivy Weir, Christina Schillaci, Kelsey Hoffman, cover designer Andie Reid, and (R.I.P.) Mr. Pringles; cover illustrator Jeremy Enecio; Brandi Bowles and Mary Pender at UTA; Richie Kern, Michael Nardullo, and Peter McGuigan at Foundry Literary + Media; Joe Barrett and Audible Studios; the independent bookstores, public libraries, and literary festivals and conferences who hosted events and signings for *Hope Never Dies: An Obama Biden Mystery*; Mala Bhattacharjee; Tiffany (the cutest wife ever), Honeytoast (the cutest kitty ever), and Buckley (a flipping jerk); and, of course, the Obamas and Bidens.

ABOUT THE AUTHOR

Andrew Shaffer is the *New York Times* best-selling author of *Hope Never Dies: An Obama Biden Mystery.* He is a two-time Goodreads Choice Awards nominee and a finalist in the Humor category. Shaffer studied comedy writing at the Second City, Chicago's famed improv school. He lives with his wife, the novelist Tiffany Reisz, in Louisville, Kentucky. He offers his sincerest apologies to the rest of the nation for Mitch McConnell. www.andrewshaffer.com